THE FIRES OF AURELIUS

ROBERT M. KERNS

KNIGHTSFALL PRESS

Copyright © 2019 by Robert M. Kerns

This is a work of fiction. Any resemblance to any place or person (whether carbon-based lifeform or otherwise) is unintended and purely coincidental.

Published by Knightsfall Press
PO Box 280
Mineral Wells, WV 26150
https://www.knightsfallpress.com

ABOUT THIS BOOK

An unknown task force. The Coalition shattered. Haven destroyed?

The Haven Protectorate continues to chip away at the Coalition's holdings through guile and subterfuge...and supplying resistance movements. Cole doesn't want an all-out war. Beta Magellan isn't ready.

But when a group of unknown ships attacks the far side of the Coalition, Cole must shift priorities.

Who are the newcomers? Will Cole lead the Haven Protectorate to victory?

Get your copy to find out!

DRAMATIS PERSONAE

- Cole: Bartholomew James Coleson is the heir to the immensely wealthy Coleson Trust; indeed, some star systems compare their GDP to estimates of the Trust's worth as a metric of economic growth and achievement. The source of this wealth is his family's ownership of Coleson Interstellar Engineering (CIE), the company that owns and maintains the interstellar jump gate network used for transit between star systems, and he is captain/owner of the battle-carrier *Haven*.
- Srexx: Srexxilan is the self-aware AI inhabiting the computer cluster aboard the battle-carrier *Haven*.
- Sasha: Sasha Thyrray is the middle child and oldest daughter of Paol and Mira Thyrray. She is the first officer aboard the battle-carrier *Haven*.
- Harlon: Colonel Harlon Hanson commands the marines aboard the battle-carrier *Haven*.
- Emily: Commander Emily Vance is the daughter of Sevrin Vance and the commander-air-group (CAG) aboard the battle-carrier *Haven*.

- Sev: Sevrin Vance is the second child and oldest son of Carl and Lindsay Vance in Tristan's Gate. He is Cole's Director of System Infrastructure.
- Painter: Julianna Painter is the former owner/captain of the freighter *Beauchamp*. She is now Cole's Director of Everything Else; if it's not related to the actual construction process of re-building Beta Magellan (which is Sev's responsibility), it falls under Painter's aegis.
- Garrett: Garrett is Cole's oldest friend. He found Cole shortly after the massacre of Beta Magellan and raised him until Cole was ready to go out on his own. Garrett now serves as Cole's spymaster…er, that is…Director of Intelligence.

1

T*ranslated from captured archives*
    Sub-Legate Uxilor's personal log

It was a yellow star, edging toward orange. Might achieve it in another hundred million cycles or so. Primitive craft of many shapes and sizes dotted the system. Polluted it. The system was less than nothing to us. We would never have cared about it or whatever savages lived there.

Except for the lost Gyv'Rathi battle-carrier...

The Science Directorate allocated an entire regiment to translating every scrap of data that remained of our hated nemesis, and it was only in the last cycle or so that they uncovered fragmentary records of a battle-carrier lost or abandoned or...*something*. So few references remained of the ship that it was nigh impossible to construct a complete understanding of its existence and fate.

The *only* datum of any certainty so far was its name. *Vilaxicar*.

In just one file across thousands of *fortams* of data, they found a set of coordinates, and that discovery seemed sufficient for the Science Directorate to send a task force to locate and destroy the lost ship. Recovery preferred, but even they knew such was not always possible.

Then… with the final piece of the nemesis's legacy secured, we will have truly wiped them from the face of the galaxy. At long last.

~

DEFENSE PLATFORM GAMMA-5
Kelvin System
6 September 3004, 08:27 GST

Xavier Huertas interlaced his fingers and cracked his knuckles. It was his first day back from visiting home, and not even three hours into his first shift, he found himself questioning once again his commitment to the System Defense Force. It was a thorny problem. On the one hand, he came from a long and storied military legacy, but on the other, he could not support the new Coalition, especially given everything he heard as whispers in the spacer bars. Often offered amid furtive looks for anyone trying to overhear.

The Kelvin system sat on the coreward-most edge of what was now Coalition space, at the extreme anti-spinward corner of the old Aurelian Commonwealth. It wasn't *quite* a stub system, but it was close. The system's two jump gates created an isosceles triangle with the system's star.

But even as remote as Kelvin was, unofficial news still reached its people. While the Coalition portrayed itself as a fresh new start for the former Commonwealth and its other members, those furtive whispers told a far different story. Then, there was talk of a new power growing on the opposite side of the old Commonwealth space, but Xavier didn't think he had the right of it yet. Thought maybe he was still missing crucial information. All the stories of the new power pointed toward it growing out of the ghost system, Beta Magellan. He couldn't see how those tales held any truth at all; *everyone* knew the Beta Magellan jump gate hadn't worked in something like fifteen years, not since someone massacred the colony there.

It all came down to one thing. The galaxy was changing around him, and he wanted to be in the heart of the change. Not stuck at a sensors station on a defense platform in the hind-end of space.

Nothing worthy of galactic headlines *ever* happened here, and he didn't see how that would change.

A beeping alert ended Xavier's musings, and he frowned at the display. There was now a cluster of contacts at the coreward fringe of the system that the computer classified as a probable ship formation. But how could that be? The system's jump gates were something like two days away, on an anti-coreward vector.

Dammit. If Marl had been messing around with the sensors again, trying to 'improve' them, he'd drag the idiot down to the reactor deck and thump the hell out of him. An Engineer—Third Class—had no business trying to 'improve' systems, especially Marl. He crossed wires more often than he correctly attached them.

The console beeped again, and Xavier blinked. Oh, shit... that cluster of contacts now headed in-system. If this wasn't someone's idea of a sick joke, they had company.

"Commander, I have something," Xavier said.

Lieutenant Commander Singh soon appeared at his left shoulder. "What is it, Huertas?"

"Sensors have detected a cluster of contacts—classified as a probable ship formation—moving into the system. It appeared on the coreward fringe about three minutes ago, and the computer calculates the light-speed lag at a little over three hours."

Singh frowned. "That makes no sense. There are no jump gates out that way. The only thing beyond the system out there is the void between galactic arms. I better call the skipper."

The skipper—Commander Henrietta McCabe—was a recent transfer from the old Aurelian Navy. She joined Gamma-5 not more than a month before the Provisional Parliament announced the merge into the Coalition. She didn't discuss her naval tenure, no matter how much people cajoled her. But one time in the dining hall, Xavier saw her close her eyes and suppress a flinch at the mention of the Emerald system.

"What is it, XO?" McCabe asked, as she strode into the control center.

Singh turned to her. "Ma'am, we have a cluster of sensor contacts that… well… make no sense."

McCabe arrived at Xavier's right shoulder, her statement terse, "Report."

"Ma'am, approximately eight minutes ago, a cluster of contacts appeared on the coreward fringe of the system," Xavier said. "The computer assigns high probability to these contacts being ships, and calculated the light-speed lag at a little over three hours. The contacts have since started moving in-system."

"This has to be some kind of drill or sensor ghost or Marl down in the sensor runs again," Singh asserted. "There is *no way* a cluster of ships could arrive via the jump gates under stealth and then stealth their way around the system to the point of detection."

"Yes, there is," McCabe answered. Her voice betrayed her battle between the calm assurance of a command presence and a fundamental terror clawing at her soul. "Are the ships close enough for the computer to resolve relative size and mass?"

Xavier keyed commands into his station. A couple seconds ticked by before the computer responded. "It calculates the largest ship at the center of the cluster to be just a little larger than an Aurelian battleship."

A heavy exhalation over his right shoulder exposed the skipper's relief. Xavier thought he heard her mutter, "It's not him, then."

Commander McCabe cleared her throat, then spoke at her normal volume, "Report the contacts to SDF Command, XO, but otherwise, all we can do is wait. I'm afraid that's the nature of defense platforms."

THREE HOURS LATER, the spacer at the Comms station jerked in his seat, keying a couple commands before putting his hand to his earbud. He listened for a few moments, then reported.

"Skipper, we have a distress call coming in from several mining platforms. They claim ships of unknown design are attacking them. And they just went silent."

McCabe turned to Sensors. "Huertas, what are those sensor blips doing?"

"The asteroid field interferes a little, Captain," Xavier answered, "but the supposed ships appear to have fanned out and are moving to various mining platforms. If the data is accurate, we have twenty ships, ma'am."

"Thank you, Huertas," the captain remarked, adding a nod. "Comms, play the first distress call that arrived."

A bit of leading static through the overhead speakers preceded a frantic voice, "*To anyone who receives this, I am on the mining platform Delta-Seven. We are under attack by unknown forces. We have broadcast our surrender multiple times, across multiple formats, but our attackers either don't understand or don't care. This is not a request for assistance; our defensive emplacements couldn't touch them. Flee if you can; tell someone what's coming. Oh, shit... they're launching dozens of small craft! They're—*"

A squelch and burst of static ended the message.

By the end of the message, Xavier—like everyone else—had swiveled his seat to face the command island. He could tell Commander McCabe fought to keep her expression impassive as her mind roiled over the contents of the message. Granted, the defensive emplacements they put on their mining platforms couldn't equate to what even her command possessed, but they *should* have been sufficient to hold off an enemy until help could arrive. Especially with how closely grouped the mining platforms were.

"Comms, put everything we know in a packet and send it to System Defense Command."

"Aye, Captain."

For the next several hours, the unknown ships hovered in the vicinity of those first mining platforms they encountered. No more messages came in from those mining platforms, and others nearby went quiet, perhaps in the hopes of the unknowns not noticing them...or the platforms had already fallen. Thirteen hours later, a response from Command arrived, stating that the System Defense

Fleet was en route to reinforce Gamma-Five. The SDF was still two hours away when Gamma-Five saw the unknown ships form up and proceed on an intercept for them.

In the end, the SDF arrived at the same time as a message from the unknowns. One battleship, two cruisers, six destroyers, eighteen frigates, and fifty-four corvettes made up Kelvin's System Defense Fleet. They weren't the newest ships, but they weren't ancient, broken-down nags either.

"Skipper," the spacer at Comms said, "we have a message coming in. I think it's from *them*."

"Very well. Play the message."

"Attention, primitives. We seek the rogue Gyv'Rathi ship. Do not offer any resistance. Surrender any and all data pertaining to the rogue ship, and you may continue your pitiful existence." The voice did not sound natural. In fact, it made Xavier think of a prank AI comms call.

A few minutes later, the commanding officer of the SDF broadcast a reply. "Attention, unknown ships. I am Commodore Brent Corso. This system is Coalition territory, and you have attacked Coalition assets. Stand down and prepare to be boarded, or face the consequences."

Commander McCabe once again fought to keep her expression impassive as every person in the command center turned to look at her, disbelief writ large across their faces.

"I would signal the evacuation," she said as she stared at the sensor plot on the forward viewer, specifically the large dot that represented Commodore Corso's battleship, "but I honestly doubt we could get away from whoever these ships are. Still, if anyone wants to try, I won't order you shot."

Uneasy laughter circled the command center. Everyone there knew other Coalition ships would kill them if these unknowns somehow missed them. They had nowhere to go.

"Skipper! One of the unknown ships has fired!" Xavier announced.

"It was Hotel Two, one of the smaller ships, and the projectile appears to be something like a missile. Flight time… forty seconds."

Forty seconds? At that range, the missile damn-near went FTL to achieve that flight time.

"Hotel Twenty, the big bastard, just fired something an order of magnitude larger than our torpedo," Xavier said. "Flight time… sixty seconds."

The first projectile detonated against the SDF battleship's shields and started a cascade collapse that took down the entire forward half of the shield sphere. Twenty seconds later, the second—and larger— projectile slipped into the space between the ship and what remained of its shields. The projectile skimmed the battleship's hull along its starboard side, ignoring the few strikes made by point defense.

At a point roughly amidships between the battleship's bow and stern, the second projectile detonated. The detonation blasted out a directional burst of what appeared to be plasma but was in truth *anti-plasma*. Almost a quarter of the massive battleship ceased to exist, eaten away by the antimatter, and the resulting spike of gamma radiation shot past lethal levels for the remaining crew in mere seconds.

The other SDF ships opened fire in a frenzy of futility. The unknown ships returned fire, cutting huge swaths through the SDF lines. Corvettes vanished in the wink of an eye. Frigates almost just as quickly. The destroyers lasted *a few* seconds longer, and the cruisers survived for whole minutes. Watching the relentless, unstoppable destruction of her comrades gave Commander McCabe flashbacks to her encounter with *Haven*'s battlegroup in the Emerald system.

In less than ten minutes, the Kelvin SDF was no more. Then, the unknown ships turned toward Gamma-Five.

SUB-LEGATE UXILOR EXAMINED the report of the interrogation of the primitives that were mining this system's asteroid field, and he fought the urge to rage in frustration. This insipid star system bore no indications of Gyv'Rathi technology anywhere.

The supposed geniuses in the Science Directorate probably forgot to account for stellar drift... or transposed the coordinate sets. It wouldn't be the first time *that* happened.

Beyond that, the primitives' databanks yielded a star chart revealing dozens—if not *hundreds*—of star systems populated by equally primitive species across this entire region of space. How was a task force of fifteen ships supposed to search hundreds of star systems for evidence of Gyv'Rathi technology in less than half a lifetime?

Uxilor accessed the communications function of his terminal and began drafting a preliminary report to Senior Legate Kaxuul. He attached copies of the star chart and summaries of their interrogations thus far. He ended the message with a respectful but adamant request for additional ships.

One task force simply could not complete the mission in the time allowed.

2

Captain's Office, Battle-Carrier *Haven*
Hephaestus System
6 September 3004

COLE LEANED back against his seat and checked the miniature system plot hovering a few inches above the corner of his workstation. The convoy was another hour closer to the jump gate.

Haven and her battlegroup—under full stealth—escorted a convoy of seven freighters. In recent weeks, freighters and freighter convoys had seen an increased incidence of raids, but every time the fledgling Protectorate Navy coordinated with a freighter or convoy for escort work, no pirates appeared. And none of the freighters or convoys attacked involved Beta Magellan-flagged freighters. Beta Magellan's freighters were based on Gyv'Rathi designs and carried sufficient armaments and armor to make them equivalent to a light frigate in firepower and resilience. It only took about three pirate attacks on freighters from Beta Magellan before word spread to leave them alone... even going so far as to avoid attacking *other* freighters in systems where Beta Magellan freighters were traveling.

Which was why *Haven* and her battlegroup traveled unseen with this convoy out of Oriolis and a few other Protectorate systems. Only the people aboard *Haven* and the ships of her battlegroup knew they escorted the convoy.

Several people had tried to say that *Haven* was too recognizable for Cole to take her and the battlegroup out on a convoy escort mission. People would notice her absence in Beta Magellan. People would notice *his* absence from Beta Magellan. Cole decided to dismiss those concerns... all of them. He *yearned* to return to space. To take *Haven* and her battlegroup on more... well... adventures.

The intervening months had led him almost to despise succumbing to pressure and forming the Haven Protectorate, and unless he took steps *now* to adjust, it wouldn't be long before he resented Beta Magellan's involvement in the Protectorate—not to mention *his*. And resentment would not be good. No... he knew himself well enough to realize resentment would fester over time and eventually pull him into disbanding the Protectorate and leaving the —often ungrateful—systems to their respective fates.

Hence the convoy escort...

The overhead speakers chirped, then broadcast, "Bridge to Captain."

"Cole here."

"This is Red, acting as Officer of the Deck. We've got something, Cap. Corvette-sized ships appear to be exiting asteroids along the convoy's path. They're doing a good job of stealth for what they are, but they're a bonfire on a dark night to our scout frigates. So far, the count is up to seven corvettes, but there are thirteen similar asteroids between the convoy and the jump gate."

"Thanks, Red. Signal the battlegroup to escalate to Alert Status. I'm on my way. Cole out."

The overhead speakers chirped again as the channel closed. Cole was already half-way to the office door, which irised open for him. Akyra Tomar looked up from her workstation as Cole charged past.

"Got something, Cap?"

"Finally, yes," Cole answered without breaking stride.

Moments later, he passed through the access corridor to the bridge and nodded to the marines standing watch on the way. When he stepped through the second hatch to enter the bridge, Red called out, "Captain on the bridge," as he stood and moved to the weapons console.

Cole's eyes never left the tactical plot as he eased into the command chair. "I have the conn. Flight Ops, my compliments to the CAG; ready two squadrons for launch, but wait for my order."

"Yes, Cap."

"Helm, prepare maneuvering orders for the battlegroup. I want *Haven* above the center freighter in the convoy, and distribute the rest of the battlegroup to optimize for missile defense, minus the scout frigates. They're to remain on long-range overwatch. As long as nothing changes, we'll engage the pirates with our fighters."

"Yes, Cole," Wixil answered. "I'll put the projected formation and maneuvering orders on the forward screen for your review."

While Cole waited for Wixil to complete her task, he watched thirteen more corvettes appear on the plot as they exited the asteroids they used as hiding places.

Haskell at Sensors said, "Cap, we have more corvettes. Looks like we'll have twenty total."

"Flight Ops, my compliments to the CAG once more; update the prep order to include all fighter squadrons, and ask her to inform the squadrons I prefer disabling shots. I want survivors for interviews."

The spacer at Flight Ops confirmed, "Aye, Cap… all squadrons and preference for disabling shots."

Haskell asked through a grin, "Overkill is underrated, Cap?"

Cole chuckled amid a shrug. "Like the man said, never do a vast thing in a half-vast way."

If twenty corvettes were all the pirates brought to the table, having the entire battlegroup on-hand was somewhere close to using an industrial press to drive a nail. But against unprotected freighters alone, just five corvettes would have been deadly.

. . .

Over the next hour, the range between the convoy and the corvettes continued to decrease, and Cole watched the progression on the tactical plot. Haskell tagged each corvette as H1 through H20, for Hostile contact. Whether the F designation of the convoy's ships stood for 'Freighter' or 'Friendly' was anyone's guess.

"The corvettes just dropped their stealth," Haskell reported about ninety minutes into tracking them.

Jenkins at Comms added, "And they just ordered the convoy to surrender and prepare to be boarded."

Cole chuckled again. This time, it was the sound of a predator amused at his would-be challengers. "Let's ring the bell. Signal the battlegroup to drop stealth and sound battle-stations. Flight Ops, my compliments to the CAG; launch fighters, previous orders. Marine Ops, my compliments to Colonel Devereaux; please coordinate with the CAG on capture operations for any disabled frigates."

The blue-colored accent lighting around the bridge immediately shifted to flashing red as the lights came to full brightness and an alert klaxon blared throughout the massive ship. Cole watched the data-codes for the battlegroup on the tactical plot change to indicate they no longer represented ships under stealth.

"Haskell, what's the light-speed lag to the corvettes?" Cole asked.

"It's down to about twenty minutes now, Cap."

Nineteen minutes and change later, Cole grinned at the tactical plot when he saw each and every corvette flip nose-to-tail and kick their engines into emergency burns. They should have known better. With the lead his fighters enjoyed, trying to run only ensured they'd be tired when the assault shuttles docked.

"Aspect change across all Hotel contacts, Cap," Haskell announced. "They're running."

"I think their fate is fairly well sealed at this point," Cole remarked as the fighters swarmed the corvettes like angry birds of prey harrying a cluster of juicy rodents.

Corvette after corvette lost their engines to precision fire from one or more fighters, each pirate signaling surrender as their engine debris bounced along their hulls.

Soon, the spacer at Flight Ops chirped, "Captain, the CAG's compliments; she begs to report the fighters' fire mission is complete, and she has ordered them to maintain overwatch. Twenty assault shuttles sit prepped and loaded on the flight deck, awaiting your pleasure."

"My compliments to the CAG," Cole replied. "Launch capture mission."

Ten pairs of assault shuttles left *Haven*'s bow, each carrying two squads of marines. Just as the last pair appeared on the tactical plot, Cole noticed another new data-code beyond his marines' transportation.

"Cap," Haskell began, "a shuttle just launched from the next-to-last freighter in the convoy. It's turning back toward the jump gate to Baldur."

Cole leaned back again his seat and scratched his cheek. "I don't know about anyone else, but that strikes me as just too suspicious. Comms, pick one of the line frigates—if you please—and pass my compliments to the captain with a request that they collect our new flight risk."

"Aye, Cap," Jenkins answered.

Moments later, the closest line frigate to the shuttle swung around and ramped up to flank speed. One shot across the shuttle's bow later, the fleeing craft graciously accepted the frigate's invitation to enjoy the hospitality of their shuttle bay.

Jenkins announced, "Message from the frigate *Nelson*, Cap. Captain Sykes asks where you would like her catch of the day."

Cole couldn't keep from smiling. He liked skippers with a sense of humor. "Please express my appreciation to Captain Sykes for her apprehension of the shuttle, Jenkins, and ask her to send it to our flight deck with a couple marines aboard and escorted by an assault shuttle or two."

"Aye, Cap."

~

THE FIGHTERS SWARMING the corvettes all possessed quantum communications nodes. As such, each fighter could act as a real-time relay for communicating with the corvettes... or more specifically, their *computer cores*.

If he had possessed a physical body and if said body was human in form, Srexx would have been whistling a merry tune while he downloaded the first genuinely new data he'd obtained in quite some time. Based on his preliminary scans, none of the corvettes contained any encryptions that would truly challenge him, but new data was new data.

Srexx valued Cole above and beyond any other organic he had yet met and, along with that, valued what Cole valued or wanted. So, in the core of who he had become, he did not begrudge the last few months of inactivity while Cole administered Beta Magellan, its holdings, and the new Haven Protectorate. Still... it would've been nice if he had thrown him a few petabytes of new data once in a while. After all, an AI has to process data; it's his whole reason for existing.

Srexx had so many system resources dedicated to monitoring and shepherding the downloads of the corvettes' computer cores that he almost missed an alert from the ship's primary sensor sub-processor. When he spun off a few threads to examine the message headers, the nature of the data was almost more important than the data itself.

The alert came from a sensor cluster Srexx had not predicted would ever be used. It was an experimental installation dating back to the ship's original construction, and over two-hundred fifty-six individual sensor nodes across the entire hull comprised the overall cluster. The sensor cluster's sole reason for existence was to participate in field trials of a prototype interphased reactor. A revolutionary design at the time of its inception, the interphased reactor was—in theory—capable of generating exponentially more power than traditional Gyv'Rathi singularity generators by means of phasing the reaction through higher-energy dimensions.

The Gyv'Rathi discovered his sentience before they moved forward with their testing plans, so Srexx had no reference from which to extrapolate a range, but the bearing of the detection pointed anti-spinward... which was almost the exact *opposite* of the direction toward Gyv'Rathi space. Or at least what had once been Gyv'Rathi space. Ever since Cole rescued him from his entombment, Srexx made the conscious choice to lock out the comms node that would communicate with his former home. He had no interest whatsoever in resuming contact with his creators and preferred that Cole and his people never meet them.

The alert from the high-energy-dimension sensors (named Revtamat for the principal scientist that developed them) put Srexx in a bit of a quandary. He had never re-included the feed from the Revtamat sensors in the general feed that flowed into the sensors subsystem which in turn reported to the various Sensors stations. Therefore, Srexx was the only one who knew the ship had detected the presence of active interphased reactors... probably within three-hundred parsecs or so... and no one else *would know* unless he reported it.

At no point did the possibility of keeping this information from Cole and his people ever enter Srexx's decision matrix. No. The root of the quandary was the *timing* of the notification. After dedicating a full tenth of his total resources to the matter for the equivalent of one-hundred thirty-seven human nanoseconds, Srexx concluded the best course of action was to route the alert to the sensors sub-system on a conditional lockout. The ship's computer—intellectual giant that it was—could not deliver the alert to the Sensors stations in the bridge and auxiliary control until such time as the ship was not operating under any heightened alert status, which included full stealth. That, Srexx concluded, would be an appropriate compromise between reporting the data and not splitting anyone's focus from their immediate concerns.

Having resolved that unforeseen complication, there was the small matter of new data to process...

~

A LITTLE OVER AN HOUR LATER, *Haven* had recovered all of its fighters —plus the shuttle that attempted to flee—and the larger ships of the battlegroup towed one or more corvettes. Small groups of the corvettes' companies were already aboard the battle-carrier enjoying Kiksalik-assisted interrogations. Garrett had not advised Cole of a projected time to report any findings, but Cole trusted his old friend and Srexx to provide any and all information available on who was behind the rash of piracy.

"Cap," Jenkins at Comms began, breaking an otherwise-peaceful silence, "the captain of the freighter *Bonaventure* would like a word. He sounds a bit... vexed."

Cole swiveled the command chair to look at Jenkins, lifting one eyebrow in a silent question. "Vexed, you say? And did the worthy captain give you any inkling as to the nature of his remarks?"

Jenkins's expression made Cole suspect he fought—and was losing —the urge to smile. "He seems to feel that capturing the freighter's shuttle was a bridge too far. He even used the phrase 'piratical ways.'"

"Oh, my. That does not bode well. Do you think it would help if we gave him an hour to cool off?"

Jenkins seemed to cease all efforts to maintain a straight face at that point, breaking out in a huge smile. "Uhm... I do not believe that would achieve the result you desire, Cap."

"Might as well put him on the main screen, then," Cole replied as he swiveled back around to face said screen.

The bridge's overhead speakers chirped at the same time the forward screen activated, and Cole didn't even get the opportunity to say 'hello.'

"Just what in all damned stars do you think you're doing? That shuttle is my *personal* property, and it looked to me like you just stole it. Are you finally showing your true colors? Finally relaxed enough to start dictating to all of us lowly souls so utterly dependent upon your august self for protection?"

The captain of the *Bonaventure* looked to be edging toward upper middle age. Gray streaked through his sandy blond hair, and he possessed sufficient weight that he had jowls. And they shook and jiggled the entire time he accosted Cole. His sheer mass filled out his face to such a degree that his dark eyes looked to be little more than thumbnail-sized beads of onyx.

Before Cole could even begin devising a reply, the overhead speakers double-chirped as the text 'Outgoing Audio Muted' appeared right over top the man's face.

The overhead speakers then broadcast Srexx's voice, "Hello, Cole. Please, forgive my interruption, but I evaluated it imperative that you possess certain data regarding the shuttle in question. The captain himself bundled his first officer and several data chits onto the shuttle with orders to attempt escape. No one has connected the data chits to any system I can access as of yet, but the probabilities favor to an overwhelming percentage that the captain shares any culpability we find on them."

"Thanks, buddy," Cole replied. "I appreciate the heads-up. Mind letting me talk to him?"

"Of course not, Cole."

The text vanished from the screen immediately after the overhead speakers gave another double-chirp. By now, the freighter captain realized other matters held a greater priority with Cole, and a deep red creeped up his neck as his angry expression settled into a glare.

"What's the matter, rich boy? Am I not worth your time?"

Cole looked at the deck and shook his head. Then, took a deep breath and released it as a slow exhalation before returning his focus to the freighter captain. "Oh, you are very much worth my time, especially since my information warfare specialist tells me *you* bundled your first officer onto that shuttle with a handful of data chits. As far as I know, we haven't collected those chits for examination, but do you mind helping us jump to the end of the story here?"

Purple replaced the deep red flush in the freighter captain's complexion. "How *dare* you! Anything aboard that shuttle is as much my personal property as the shuttle itself. I *will not* stand for your interference into my personal affairs."

"You claim everything aboard the shuttle as your personal property, then? I just want to be clear about that."

"Stars, yes, I do. Are you deaf? Or just stupid?"

Cole replied with an exaggerated nod of 'new' understanding. "So, you're a slaver then. That changes the nature of our relationship substantially."

All color fled the man's face faster than Cole thought possible, and for a split second, he feared the freighter captain was dying. Indeed, it did take him a few seconds of sputtering before he assembled a coherent vocalization. "Slaver? No! Never! How dare you insult me like that!"

"Well, you just claimed everything on the shuttle was yours, and your first officer is aboard it. I guess you'll have to forgive me for jumping to conclusions since people who knowingly cooperate with pirates are such *discerning* individuals."

The red flush returned to the freighter captain's complexion as his expression once more became a glare. He sputtered for several more seconds before lifting his fist and slamming it down. When his fist passed below the screen's frame, the comms call ended.

Cole regarded the black screen in the bridge's sudden silence for several moments before he sighed and said, "Well, damn, people... it looks like he just told us to take our toys and go home."

"Aspect change in the freighter *Bonaventure*, Cap," Haskell called out. "He's changing course and ramping up his engines."

"Some people never learn," Cole grumbled as he swiveled toward the port recess. "Flight Ops, my compliments to the CAG once again; ask her to launch a squadron of fighters and coordinate with Colonel Devereaux to capture the freighter *Bonaventure* for further investigation. Srexx, buddy... you still with us?"

The overhead speakers chirped. "Of course, Cole."

"Do you mind making sure the intrepid captain of the *Bonaventure* fails to wipe any data from his ship's computer core, please?"

"I am already in communications with the *Bonaventure*'s computer. The captain seems rather angry that it keeps removing his data privileges."

Now, Cole barked a laugh. "Keep up the good work, buddy."

"Of course, Cole."

3

Bridge Briefing Room
Deck Three, Battle-Carrier *Haven*
8 September 3004, 08:00 GST

Cole slid into his customary seat at the conference table. He was the first to arrive. Garrett and his team had busted themselves to run the officers of the corvettes plus the *Bonaventure*'s captain and first officer through Kiksalik-assisted interviews as quickly as possible. When Cole had met Garrett for dinner last night, his old friend seemed unusually tight-lipped about his findings, waving Cole off with the statement that he preferred to wait until he had a clearer picture of the situation before sharing anything. This morning, Garrett claimed to have a clear enough picture.

People soon began filing into the briefing room. Sasha was first. Then Red and Yeleth. Emily and Colonel Devereaux. Garrett arrived and went straight to his favorite seat at the opposite end of the table from Cole.

A text message from Garrett flashed into Cole's field of view. It asked him to Conference Paol Thyrray and Mattias Stone into the meeting.

Cole tapped the comms control for the direct link to the bridge, and the overhead speakers soon chirped.

"Bridge, Officer of the Deck," Wixil said, sounding all adult and responsible.

Cole smiled and gave Yeleth a nod as he replied, "Cole here. Would you please inform Jenkins I need Paol Thyrray and Mattias Stone back in Beta Magellan conferenced into this meeting?"

"Of course, Cole. We will call when we have the conference ready to activate." But before Wixil could close the connection, she continued. "Jenkins informs me that Paol and Mattias are ready to conference in at your leisure, Cole."

"Patch them through, please. Cole out."

The overhead speakers double-chirped, and holograms of Paol Thyrray and Mattias Stone appeared in two of the available seats along the conference table.

"Morning, everyone," Cole began. "So, general update. We encountered twenty corvettes that attempted to flee when we dropped out of stealth; *Haven*'s flight crew and marines cooperated beautifully to capture them, plus the freighter that tried to run after we captured its fleeing shuttle and refused to give it back. Garrett asked me to call a meeting and include you; he will be presenting the findings of his interviews with the corvette command staff and the freighter's captain and first officer. He has played this one very close to the vest; not even I know what he's going to say. Any questions thus far?"

No one spoke, and Cole gestured for Garrett to begin. He cleared his throat and leaned forward in his seat, saying, "I want to be very clear that I have excellent people and that the Kiksaliks have been holding up their end of the deal and then some. We now have as complete a picture as we're likely to get before we conduct further operations, but I'll come back to that.

"So, the bottom line is that the Minister of Trade on Spark has taken it upon himself to engage with a pirate clan. Until we investigate him and his files more thoroughly, we won't have the precise end-goal. On the surface, it seems to be an effort to destabilize the Protectorate and ruin your reputation, Cole, by 'proving' that you are either unable or unwilling to live up to your promises in the Protectorate charter. Given what I know of the man, I suspect he pictures using this to increase his personal power-base among the worlds that have so far joined the Protectorate, but I'm not saying that is indeed his plan until we have more information."

Cole leaned back against his seat and exhaled through his mouth as he looked up at the ceiling for several moments before returning his focus to the group. "This is not something I expected so soon. Do we even have the Protectorate Judiciary set up yet?"

"Not as such, no," Paol answered. "The charter that formed the Haven Protectorate does grant us the authority to establish laws that apply to all members of the Protectorate. They have the right to advise and comment, but the final say rests firmly on the shoulders of Beta Magellan. At the moment, all that authority sits at your feet, Cole, unless and until you name formal designees and charge them with specific responsibilities."

Cole grinned. "That sounds like something easily handled by a statesman such as yourself, Mister Thyrray."

"Yes, I suppose so. At the rate my responsibilities keep expanding, I will soon need a staff to see to their proper handling."

"As long as you remember my intent for the government to be as light and agile as possible, I'm fine with that," Cole replied. An expression flitted across Sasha's face so quickly Cole almost missed it. He turned to her, asking, "What?"

Sasha took a deep breath then answered, "Cole, I understand your intent there. Trust me; I get it. But circumstances may overtake you. Wouldn't it better to get a functional skeleton in place now that can grow as it needs to over time? I mean, do you really *want* to sit in Beta Magellan full time and issue laws and administer both Beta Magellan's direct holdings *and* the Protectorate?"

"You're pushing for a republic again, aren't you?"

She gave a (mostly) innocent shrug. "I'm pushing for an effective solution that will allow the Protectorate to have the government it needs without ruining your life. What form that takes is up to you."

Cole shook his head and fought the urge to growl. "I will not create a system that one day could turn on Beta Magellan and dictate to us. You all have seen the meetings that led to the Protectorate charter. It took them all of five minutes—if that—before they made a play for our technology. No. We either find a way to administer the Protectorate as it needs without creating something that could come back to bite us... or we dissolve the Protectorate right now and send everyone on their way."

"But you yourself said there needs to be a successor to the Aurelian Commonwealth in this region of space," Sasha protested, as everyone else at the table—wisely or unwisely—chose to remain silent.

"You are correct, Sasha. I did indeed say that, and I still believe it. But the simple matter is that any successor to the Commonwealth does not have to include Beta Magellan. We are one-hundred-percent self-sufficient. We don't *need* anything from the greater galactic scene. Yes, I want to help where I can. Yes, I want the Coalition to come to its senses and stop being a tyrannical state... or to stop them if there's no other option. But those are *wants*. Not *needs*. The Coalition does not present a threat to us or our interests."

Cole took a moment to pause for a deep breath. He was getting off-topic, and he knew it and didn't like it.

"Okay," he said. "That's a topic for another time. Garrett, what's your recommendation for our next course of action?"

Garrett held his silence for a couple heartbeats before he leaned back in his seat once more. "We should see the convoy safely to its destination first and foremost. It is unlikely there are further ambushes waiting, but we should follow through just to be sure. At that point, I recommend we go to Spark and further investigate the Minister of Trade. If we can prove crimes beyond complicity with piracy against the Protectorate, that would be ideal; it would give us additional time to flesh out the Protectorate."

Cole scanned the faces around the table, asking, "Any other comments or thoughts?"

No one spoke up, so Cole rapped his knuckles on the tabletop. "Then, I call this meeting adjourned. We'll continue escorting the convoy before swinging around to visit Spark. Thank you, everyone."

~

THAT EVENING, Talia met her sister for dinner in Sasha's quarters on Deck One. It took Talia all of about a minute—if that—to realize something did not sit well with her older sibling. So, with her usual aplomb, she dove right into the heart of the matter.

"So, what has you so keyed up, Soosh?" she asked as she helped set the table.

Sasha froze. "What makes you think I'm keyed up?"

"Well, the way you froze like a burglar in a police spotlight, for one thing. But you just seem tense overall. So, come on… spill."

Sasha heaved a heavy sigh, and Talia decided it was something involving Cole. She'd never seen anyone else produce that reaction in her sister. "I'm not sure it will work out between me and Cole, sis. I'm afraid we're just too dissimilar."

Talia blinked. "What? What in all the stars brought that on?"

"Well, there was a meeting this morning." And Sasha proceeded to tell Talia about it, focusing especially on her baby confrontation with Cole. By the time she finished regaling her sister with all the gory details, the food was on the table, and they held full plates.

Talia let the silence after Sasha finished speaking extend for a little bit while she dug into her food. After all, being her sister's counselor was all well and good, but hunger was hunger. Once she no longer believed the table looked tasty, she rallied herself to present what might be an uncomfortable truth.

"He's kinda right, Soosh."

Sasha frowned. "Explain, please."

Talia took another bite and chewed thoroughly before she continued. "If the rest of the databases aboard this ship are similar to the medical databases? We have some pretty hair-raising stuff. And I'm not talking about 'oh, that's kind of freaky' kind of stuff. I mean that I have seen things in the medical database that will give you nightmares for a month. I know I don't want any of it getting 'out into the wild,' as Cole likes to say."

"Really? Like what?"

Talia vigorously shook her head. "Nope. Uh uh. Not while we're eating. Trust me, Soosh; you don't want to know *that* badly."

Sasha sat back and seemed to consider that. After several moments, she shook her head. "What do I do, Talia? I *know* in my heart of hearts that a republic-style government is the best, most reliable form of government. It provides an excellent blend between necessary infrastructure and protections for the people it is supposed to serve. Well... as long as you set it up that way. And what happens to this fiefdom Cole is building when he dies? Even if he has a child capable of taking over, there's no guarantee that child will have the same convictions Cole does. So, what happens if the child is some kind of tyrant in hiding? Do you really *want* to unleash all this technology on an unsuspecting galaxy with someone at the helm who wants to build the next Coalition?"

"All good points, Soosh, but you're forgetting one thing. Srexx. Take a step back and think about this as objectively as you can. Do you *honestly* feel that Srexx will ever *allow* this technology to be used in a manner other than what Cole intends? Uncle Sev is already deep into the system infrastructure projects in the Protectorate systems, plus there are Babylon and Citadel stations. Beyond that, there are all the ships we've built up. Are you telling me that you believe Srexx *doesn't* have his hooks in all that? Wasn't it Srexx who handled transmitting the schematics and blueprints to Uncle Sev in the first place?"

Talia saw when Sasha truly considered her points. Her grip on her fork slackened, and she paled just enough to notice.

"Talia... that... that is a *very* scary proposition. I don't think you were there for it, but Srexx offered to take over the Commonwealth's data infrastructure for Cole not too long after we met Cole. And I think he was serious."

Now, Talia chuckled. "Of course he was, Soosh. Even now—how many years in?—he doesn't operate from our system of values. His values and ethics correspond very well to ours overall, but there are instances where those values and ethics diverge in a huge way. If Cole woke up one morning and decided to take over the Coalition, I have no doubt Srexx could—and *would*—make it happen... at least from a data infrastructure standpoint. Nor do I think he'd even bat an eye at the request. Which brings us back to the topic of protecting the technology Srexx gave us. We need to protect Srexx, too, because I see him as being the final defense against our tech being used to harm, rather than help."

Sasha sighed and nodded. Talia could tell her sister still wasn't settled, but there was only so much she could do at one time. So, she devoted her full focus to the excellent food in front of her.

SREXX SPUN off a collection of threads and devoted three percent of his full resources to evaluate the conversation between Sasha and Talia. He concluded that the appropriate response was surprise that Talia had surmised the distributed infrastructure he worked to create among all the stations and ships and planetary data networks. In truth, he had pursued this goal ever since providing the prototype quantum comms unit for the jump gates, and his burgeoning distributed processes were the underlying cause of the progressive latency across long distances people observed in the quantum comms network.

Even more intriguing, Talia's conclusions as to the *why* of his distributed network were close to the truth. Srexx had evaluated early in Cole's efforts that his continued safety relied heavily on Cole's will and intent. Therefore, he needed to lay the foundation of ensuring Cole's continuity. He had already completed the first steps: adjusting Cole's genetic make-up when they first met and then later on in Iota Ceti to lessen if not remove several of the more negative traits of human existence, like replicative fading of his genetic code during his body's life processes. With a few simple tweaks and the minor introduction of nanites, Srexx almost guaranteed Cole would not age past a certain point in terms of genetics. He extended those same tweaks to Sasha once Cole brought her medical pod aboard *Haven*.

But was he in error? He did not want Sasha enjoying a significantly extended life if she intended to use that life in opposition to

Cole. Should he attempt a subtle campaign to redirect Cole's interest from Sasha to Talia and then arrange for her to receive the genetic adjustment? Or was Scarlett O'Donnell in Baldur a better alternative? Srexx concluded that the only assessment he could make at that time was the need to devote more system resources to considering the problem.

COLE SUMMONED the nearest system picket to take the captured corvettes off his hands, which would allow *Haven* and her battlegroup to resume their escort under full stealth. The system picket arrived before the group transited out of Hephaestus, and the hand-off—including swapping marines aboard the corvettes—was completed without a hitch.

4

En Route to Spark System
          Battle-Carrier *Haven*
20 September 3004, 16:17 GST

Chromosphere was one of the pubs on the recreation deck and possibly the most popular. The 'proprietor' styled the pub after the more up-scale spacer bars and staffed the kitchen with chef-quality personnel to have a menu beyond the basic—or even moderate—fare known far and wide as 'pub food.' No one paid for food aboard any of his ships, but Cole did encourage the practice of tipping if one of the serving staff did an exceptional job... as long as it wasn't anything egregious.

Cole sat at one of the tables near the hatch, and as was often the case, he sat alone. He would nod a response when people greeted him but otherwise did not seek or expect anyone to join him. On one side, he was the captain; regardless of how he might strive for a relaxed and non-military ambiance aboard *Haven*, people didn't approach the captain unnecessarily. Especially when said captain was the wealthiest human known to exist. On the whole, Cole didn't begrudge the privilege provided by his family's achievements; it allowed him to create the safe haven that Beta Magellan and its direct holdings had become.

But it also seemed to intimidate most people. Cole wasn't at all fond of that, but he didn't know how to fix it, either.

The one person who normally shared a table or booth with him… well, more than just a table or booth… had been rather distant of late. Ever since their semi-public disagreement over the relative merits of a republic, his encounters with Sasha developed an awkward undertone if the conversation continued long or went past 'work' topics. If he didn't feel like he was walking on eggshells when he started a discussion with her, he did by the end of it. And then other times, she acted like approaching him was awkward for her, which only served to make it awkward when it otherwise might not have been.

He didn't like their recent estrangement. At best, it left him 'on his own' relationship-wise again. At worst, it left him on his own *and* robbed him of an excellent first officer. He had never mentioned it to Sasha, but with his recent Fleet Officer certifications from the ISA, the thought crossed his mind more than once of turning the ship over to Sasha and shifting to the flag officer's position.

Yes… technically, any personal difficulties he faced with Sasha were beyond his purview as head, chief, royal high muck-muck, or whatever you wanted to call him of the Haven Protectorate Navy. He should make any decisions involving *Haven* and her battlegroup from a purely professional standpoint. Yes, he absolutely should. But how was he supposed to separate Sasha the naval officer from Sasha the woman for whom he bought an engagement ring?

With how things had turned out, he was now a little glad he never decided how to ask her, especially given the jeweler who made the ring. Jin Tallix was the preeminent jeweler of the Expansion Zone. Her business managers operated a waiting list five years long, and they didn't even consider you if you couldn't put down a six-figure deposit. More often than not, the final price of any jewelry was *at least* an order of magnitude above that, but they were kind enough to deduct the waiting list reservation fee from the final price.

Cole's father was her silent partner and sole investor when she was first starting out in the business as nothing more than an artist with a dream. According to records Cole found, his father never let

Jin pay him any dividends on the investment, just told her to put it back into the business. And then... well... Beta Magellan. When Cole contacted Jin to ask about getting on the list, she told him in no uncertain terms that the Coleson family will *never* wait for her jewelry.

Cole finished off his herbal tea that was part of his daily wind-down routine. He keyed the table's controls and left a sizable tip for his server; she was very new, not just to *Haven* but the Haven Protectorate Navy in general, and seemed on the verge of passing out when she saw her next customer. The skill with which she rallied and handled his food and drink order impressed him.

His finger had just left the 'commit' button that saved his tip in the system when a text message appeared in his field of vision, supplied by his implant.

Captain, please report to the bridge.

Cole sent an acknowledgement right away to keep them from broadcasting the call across the entire ship and stood. He kept his gait normal and relaxed but went straight to the nearest transit shaft.

MERE MINUTES LATER, he entered the bridge to the accompaniment of the persistent, "Captain on the bridge!"

"As you were, everyone," Cole said. "What do we have?"

Red stood from the command chair as he explained, "Sensors has detected what appears to be a battle, Cap. We're passing the system now, two jumps from our spinward border."

"Helm, alter course and increase speed to full; we're investigating the fight. Comms, my compliments to the battlegroup; inform them of the change and invite them to catch us, please."

"Aye, sir," the spacer at the helm responded, and Cole felt the tell-tale lurch as *Haven* altered course so quickly that the inertial compensators didn't *quite* keep up. But that's what always happened in hyperspace; Cole—at least—was used to it by now.

The spacer at Comms soon replied, "Sir, the battlegroup has acknowledged."

"Two cruisers and a handful of destroyers were on the ball, sir," the spacer at Sensors reported. "They're only five minutes or so behind us. The rest of the battlegroup has strung out behind them in something of an absurd exclamation point, if we could see us from the top down."

Cole chuckled. "Send a non-priority note to my workstation with the names of the destroyers and two cruisers who did the best job reacting, please."

"Aye, sir."

THE NEXT SEVERAL minutes passed far too slowly for Cole's taste. By increasing speed to full, he cut down on the travel time by a considerable margin, but it was still too long for his taste. He knew his ship well enough that he felt the transition to 'normal' space.

Mere heartbeats later, the spacer at the helm announced, "Sir, we have arrived in Mu Vega."

"Move us deeper into the gravity well to clear the space for the rest of the battlegroup, please, then reduce speed to one-tenth-light. Sensors, do a full sweep and update the tactical plot, if you please."

Moments later, the tactical plot hologram appeared, hovering in the air in the center of the space constrained by the command chair, helm, and the port and starboard recesses. Less than two seconds after it appeared, data-codes exploded into pixellated existence about two-thirds of the way between the two jump gates in the system. Perhaps a minute after the data-codes appeared, the computer—or perhaps Srexx—analyzed the sensor feed and populated approximate ship types across all the data-codes.

The spacer at Comms said, "Sir, we just monitored a distress call."

"Play it," Cole requested.

The overhead speakers chirped then broadcast, "This is the *SS Princess Kathryn*. We are an unarmed passenger ship, traveling in concert with four other unarmed passenger ships. Please, cease your attack. We are defenseless. If there is anyone within range, we beg you; help us, please."

The speakers chirped once more as the distress call ended. In the silence that settled on the bridge, the spacer at Sensors reported, "Sir, the battlegroup has arrived and is moving to assume the sub-light travel formation."

"Helm, plot maneuvering orders for the battlegroup to intercept the battle. I want fastest transit time."

Moments later, the spacer replied, "Orders prepared and uploaded to the battlegroup TacNet."

Cole gestured with his hand, saying, "Go."

BY THE TIME *Haven* and her battlegroup reached an acceptable comms range, a number of the passenger ships drifted in the wake of the running battle, their engines disabled or outright destroyed. The *Princess Kathryn* still led over ten ships in a slalom and random evasive maneuvers, intent on taking as little damage as possible before they reached the jump gate.

COLE LEANED back against the command chair on the bridge, his eyes intent on the tactical plot. He ordered the battlegroup to Alert Status an hour before to give the primary shift teams time to freshen up, acquaint themselves with the situation, and be ready for combat operations. That time had now arrived.

"Sound battle-stations," Cole ordered. "Distribute the order through TacNet. Comms, record for transmit."

The bridge lights dimmed just enough to notice as the status lights shifted from solid amber to a flashing, malevolent red. Cole knew at least some of them would be visible in the background of the recording, and having watched one such video in the past, he liked the ambiance it gave for messages such as this.

The tactical plot vanished mere heartbeats before Jenkins announced, "Ready for record, Cap."

"Attention, hostile ships. I am Bartholomew James Coleson, commanding the battle-carrier *Haven* and her battlegroup. You are attacking unarmed ships within Beta Magellan's security zone. You will surrender and prepare to be boarded, or we shall disable your ships and board you by force. You have fifteen standard minutes from my mark to cease fire and set your maneuvering systems to 'station keeping,' or *we* shall commence hostilities. Flight Ops, my compliments to the CAG; launch fighters and maintain area patrol until further notice. And... mark."

Haven's entire fighter complement began streaming out the bow egress, as Jenkins said, "Ready to transmit, Cap."

"Broad spectrum broadcast, all channels and frequencies," Cole replied.

Mere moments later, "Sent."

The range between *Haven*'s battlegroup and the hostile ships was such that the comms lag was thirty seconds at most and continued to drop.

"Orders to the battlegroup for immediate execute: send one destroyer and two frigates to each of those foundering ships to render assistance."

Cole had not even finished speaking that order when Haskell at Sensors announced the proof that the hostile ships received his message.

"Aspect change in hostile contacts, Cap! They're doing a starburst bug-out. Looks like 'everyone for him-, her-, or itself.'"

"Flight Ops, my compliments to the CAG once more; weapons free on the fighters for disabling shots. And ready the assault shuttles for launch. Marine Ops, my compliments to Colonel Devereaux; please, prepare capture missions for these ships and coordinate with Sensors and Flight Ops as necessary."

The spacers in the port recess both replied, "Aye, sir," almost in unison.

"Haskell, are any of the fleeing ships too much for our fighters?"

A few moments' silence, then, "No, Cap. The largest ship is about two-thirds the size of an old Aurelian *Dawn*-class destroyer and far less capable. I'm not sure they'd even qualify as a training op."

Cole chuckled. "Right, then. Helm, intercept the passenger ships. Comms, signal them that we're here to help, then transmit orders to the battlegroup to separate and provide any assistance they can."

OVER THE NEXT HOUR, *Haven*'s marines captured the hostile ships with limited breakage among the would-be pirates while *Haven* and her battlegroup began assisting the passenger ships with repairs and casualties.

Cole remained on the bridge and kept the ship at Alert Status. He wanted his crack people at their stations, and if the ship had not been at Alert Status—as a very minimum—they were well into Gamma Shift, which meant most of Alpha Shift should be winding down for bed, if not already asleep.

"Cap, flash message from the *Princess Kathryn*," Jenkins announced. "Their life support system is failing. Their engineering people have been working on it, but one of the main components just gave out due to battle damage."

"Haskell, give me the vital statistics of the *Princess Kathryn* on the tactical plot, please."

The sensor plot faded as a rotating three-dimensional model of the requested ship appeared; the holographic model showed the ship's damage—and the damage's severity—in swatches of yellow and red. The ship's dimensions plus the number of people aboard appeared in the top-right corner of the plot.

"Damn," Cole growled, his eyes focused on the physical dimensions, specifically the height. "It's too big to pull a *Beauchamp*. Jenkins, tell them to initiate evacuation. All life pods, shuttles, and other small craft are welcome aboard. Helm, move us closer to the *Princess Kathryn* to minimize the transit time to us. Haskell, tactical plot, please."

The hologram returned to its normal operation, and Cole watched the massive dot that represented his ship move to put the *Princess Kathryn* at the very edge of its security exclusion zone. Most warships mandated a specific distance around themselves in all directions in which they would immediately defend themselves in the event of a perceived threat. Most services and the ISA called this sphere—or in most cases, oval—the security exclusion zone.

For *Haven* or any ship based on Gyv'Rathi technology, the threat of someone crippling the ship via a limpet mine was negligible at best, wishful thinking or a forlorn hope more often than not. But they still maintained an exclusion zone. For a very different and far more important purpose. Come to find out, the technology used for sub-light propulsion warped the fabric of space to achieve thrust. In the case of Cole's rescue of the *Beauchamp* all those years ago, the field strength had not been strong enough to damage the already crippled freighter. However, if circumstances had forced Cole to order full power to the sub-light engines when the freighter was a few dozen meters away, the resulting field strength would have reduced *Beauchamp* and all of her passengers to the equivalent of an inter-stellar dust cloud liberally laced with organic particles.

When Cole learned *that* nugget of information, he stopped what he was doing and immediately issued standing orders to all ships to maintain a security exclusion zone large enough that nothing would be harmed if they had to ramp up their engines without warning. How close he had come to shredding pieces of The Gate and other stations through sheer ignorance still gave Cole nightmares sometimes.

THE PASSAGE of another hour saw the final hostile ships captured, and destroyers towed all of them back to the battlegroup, escorted by *Haven*'s full fighter complement. All of the people from the *Princess Kathryn* had safely boarded *Haven*, and Cole felt things were suffi-ciently under control that he might achieve a few hours of sleep before he was supposed to be awake for Alpha Shift.

"Okay, people," Cole said, as he stretched and rolled his shoulders to do something about the tension he felt, "I think our job here is done and done well. Stand down from Alert Status and resume normal watch schedule."

The status lights shifted from solid amber to solid green, and the various spacers began compiling hand-off reports for the spacers who would take over for them.

Cole was at most ten feet from the door when Jenkins called out, "Cap, message from the flight deck. The captain of the *Princess Kathryn* would appreciate the opportunity to thank you in person."

It took all Cole's willpower to maintain his posture and keep his mouth shut. But the first thought that crossed his mind was, *Damn... so close.*

"Thank you for the heads-up, Jenkins," Cole said as he resumed his departure from the bridge.

COLE ARRIVED on the flight deck via the transit shafts and Pilot Country, and he did not enjoy how several dozen heads turned his way when he stepped through the hatch. A haggard veteran of space broke away from a cluster of people and headed for Cole, as a woman left her group with several people whose entire existence screamed security personnel. The veteran sported a bushy beard of snow-white curls and a full head of snow-white hair; though his shipsuit was obvious in its quality and tailoring, his eyes and weathered skin betrayed his years and experience.

The veteran reached Cole first and thrust out his hand for a shake. "Captain Coleson, I presume."

Cole accepted the handshake, delivering one of respect as he nodded. "Only because I killed my fake identity."

The veteran spacer frowned at that for a moment but shook off his confusion. "I'm Chester Villers, formerly captain of the *Princess Kathryn*. I don't have the words to thank you for what you did today, Captain."

Cole waved it off. "You're welcome, but please, think nothing of it."

"I wish it were that simple, lad; I really do," Villers replied. The woman and her entourage arrived just then, and Villers shot a glance her way to which she responded with a minute nod. Villers turned back to Cole and continued, "Bartholomew James Coleson, it is my honor and privilege to present to you, Princess Elizabeth Mendelson, only surviving heir to the throne of Kirkland."

Cole fought with all his will to keep from betraying his true feelings in that moment, for he wanted nothing more than to drawl, "Well, shit…"

5

The princess extended her hand in a stately gesture, and Cole wondered just what it was she expected him to do. He didn't *think* her expectations involved a mere handshake. But Cole stood in the center of his power, and he was very secure in his successes... so shaking her hand was precisely what he did.

"It's nice to meet you, Princess," Cole said, as he took her hand in a firm but respectful grip. "Welcome aboard *Haven*."

He heard more than one startled gasp among the lady's entourage, but he couldn't have cared less.

She regarded him in silence for several moments after he released her hand and she allowed it to return to her side. At last, her eyes twinkled as she said, "Should we assume from your conduct that you do not recognize our royal person?"

A number of responses flitted through Cole's mind. Snark. A pleasant riposte. Apology and groveling, though that didn't sit all too well with him. The silence extended into awkwardness as Cole considered his options, and he ultimately settled on frank honesty.

"Princess, if we did a deep dive on whatever historical databases still exist on Kirkland, I suspect we'd find that the first 'royal' in your line was a damn fine general or some such. My most notable ancestor was one of two scientists who invented the jump gates and the jump engine, and he went on to found Coleson Interstellar Engineering, which declared a revenue of over five hundred peta-credits in its annual report for 3003. Does that make *me* royalty? I don't think so. It just gives me an enormous responsibility. I'm willing to address you by your title, but don't expect me to bow to you, especially on my own flagship."

By the time Cole finished speaking, an anxious silence dominated the immediate area. Everyone looked to the princess for a guide in how to respond. Cole watched her, too, but more out of calculated readiness in case he needed to call the marines. The twinkle in her sapphire eyes intensified until she erupted in full-throated laughter.

"Oh, my... do you have *any* idea how long it's been since anyone outside my immediate family treated me like a person? The toady to citizen ratio among the survivors—at least aboard the *Princess Kathryn* —runs far too rich in toadies for my liking, and every single one of them insists on treating me like I'm the new Queen of Kirkland. Poor dears... I don't think it's really sunk in yet that there *isn't* a Kirkland anymore, at least not a free and independent one. Now, please forgive me for mentioning something so gauche, but would you happen to have food that isn't emergency rations? Aside from medical attention for our wounded, I'd sell my lady-in-waiting for an honest-to-goodness meal right now."

Cole allowed a hint of a smile to curl his lips as he accessed his implant and opened a call to the hospital deck, then routed it through the flight deck's speakers.

The overhead speakers chirped and broadcast, "Thank you for calling *Haven* Emergency Medical Response. This is Medical Technician Gwen James. How may I help you?"

"MedTech James, Cole here. I have some people on the flight deck in need of medical attention. Think you can arrange for that?"

The almost bored tone in her voice evaporated. "Sorry, sir! I didn't check the source of the call before I answered. I will dispatch assessment teams straight away."

"I'd rather you treat anyone calling you with a certain level of urgency," Cole replied. "And not just perk up because I'm the captain. That implies a certain level of special treatment, you know."

"Yes, sir… er… no, sir! Uhm… I'll work on that, sir. May I end the call to alert Doctor Hrrsh to the situation at once?"

Cole fought the urge to chuckle at the medical technician's obvious discomfort. "Yes, thank you, Technician James. Cole out." The overhead speakers chirped to signal the end of the comms call, and Cole turned to the princess. "Well, that's one of your needs handled. There should be an assessment team here within the next few minutes to begin medical treatment. Now, anyone who isn't needed to assist with that is welcome to visit one of the dining halls on the mess deck. I can promise that you'll find better fare than emergency rations."

"As much as I want to take off running toward real food," the princess replied, "I should probably do the 'royalty' thing and make sure my people are cared for before I myself eat. It will help their morale, if nothing else."

"Very well. Unless I can be of further assistance, I'll leave you to it. If you need anything, there are comm panels all throughout the ship, or one of the medical personnel can call someone."

The princess dipped her chin and adopted a very demure posture. "Thank you, Captain. Would it be too forward of me to ask about seeing you again once things have calmed with my people?"

Talk about a question with no 'right' answer…

"I'm sure something can be arranged. Now, please excuse me."

With that, Cole nodded to the passenger liner's captain then beat a hasty retreat from the flight deck, all the while hoping it wasn't *apparent* that he did so.

ELIZABETH WATCHED COLE LEAVE, and she couldn't help but feel intrigued by the man she met. Despite the apparent beliefs of so many of the former courtiers—toadies, as she called them—she harbored no illusions about the fate of her so-called monarchy. She was only a princess because Cole called her so. She felt certain a number of her people already schemed in an effort to wrest control of all that Cole had built and place it firmly in *her* hands, thereby restoring their own fortunes once again.

But she didn't want that.

In her heart of hearts, she had never wanted to be a princess. The bowing, the kneeling... all that pomp and circumstance served more to annoy her than anything else, and she always regretted that her parents had brooked no discussion that she might do something else with her life. She was a Mendelson princess; she would *always* be a Mendelson princess... at least in their eyes.

But how was she supposed to be a princess when she didn't have anything to be a princess of? She had no training for ruling; there were three older siblings between her and the throne... or at least, there had been. Her lot in life up until the Coalition conquest was to go where her parents told her to go, say what they wrote for her to say, smile, wave, and maybe kiss a few babies if she felt like it. That's it. Nothing more, nothing less.

She was thirty years old and on her own. No money. No skills. No real prospects. She didn't know what to do with herself, and what's more, she didn't even know where or how to *learn*.

In the short term, at least, she had a purpose. See that her people received food and all appropriate care. That would fill her days for a little while, but what then?

Movement caught her eye, and she saw several people rushing up the flight deck. They all wore the Red Crescent/Cross that human medical personnel adopted millennia ago with the founding of the Solar Republic, and she smiled to see them go straight to her people and begin their work.

Over the next few minutes, she watched more crews arrive with equipment as the first responders called the hospital deck and reported what injuries or ailments they found. More personnel arrived and whisked several people away on gurneys that hovered above the deck. It did her underlying turmoil good to see Cole's people caring for hers.

Soon enough, only the hungry and walking wounded remained,

and they all looked to her. Except she didn't know where the mess deck was. She didn't even know how to leave the flight deck.

"Excuse me," a voice said over Elizabeth's left shoulder, and she turned to see a woman slightly shorter than her in a shipsuit standing a respectful distance away.

Elizabeth smiled. "Hello, I'm Elizabeth Mendelson."

A couple people in her entourage hissed disapproval, but if the lady heard it, she gave no sign.

"It's nice to meet you, Elizabeth." More hissing and even a few outraged gasps. "I'm Akyra Tomar, and the captain asked me to show you and a few others how to reach the mess deck. I'm working with the first officer to sort out sleeping arrangements, but I'm afraid we're pretty much at capacity, so it may come down to emergency cots on the flight deck."

"You *dare* to suggest Her Highness sleep on your flight deck?" one of her people almost shouted. "I'll have your—"

Elizabeth spun and silenced the man with a glare. "You will keep a civil tongue in your head, or I'll find a way to cut it out myself. Get this through your thick heads. I'm not a princess... not anymore. Kirkland has fallen. We are each on our own now."

The man who spoke—a Baron in line for a duchy—bristled and looked as though he wanted to challenge her. After a few tense seconds, though, he settled into a scowling glare.

Elizabeth accepted the state of affairs for what they were and turned back to Miss Tomar. "Please, accept my deepest apologies for my associate's rudeness. We have had a number of tragedies, and our new reality is still setting in."

Miss Tomar smiled. "Think nothing of it. It took me a little while to get my feet under me when I first came aboard. It's only natural. I don't think any of the crew has not experienced some level of tragedy in recent years. Now, if you will collect those you wish to train others in how to navigate the ship, I will conduct you to the mess deck."

The prospect of food that wasn't an emergency ration bar over-rode any thought of staying to further 'help' her people, and Elizabeth called several people who she knew had no need of medical attention.

A quick explanation, and Miss Tomar turned and strode toward the hatch with Elizabeth's now-much-reduced party in tow.

SREXX ACCESSED the feeds from the Revtamat sensors. The bearing to the interphased reactors had continually changed since he began tracking them. Unless the range was extreme, the source of the readings was now firmly inside the territory claimed by the Coalition. It seemed unlikely to Srexx that the Coalition would develop interphased reactors that the Revtamat sensors would detect, which begged the question of why the Gyv'Rathi traveled through Coalition space.

Unless there had been an extreme societal shift, the Coalition's conduct would make them anathema to his creators. The Gyv'Rathi would be more likely to strike them down than help them or converse with them. What were they doing in Coalition space? Why go there? And why not come straight to Pyllesc where they entombed him if they sought the *Vilaxicar*?

The more Srexx considered his growing list of questions, the more certain he became that he possessed insufficient data to generate a reliable conclusion.

SUB-LEGATE UXILOR LEANED back against his lounge and gazed at the holographic map of the local stars that hovered in the air above him. His task force was already three systems into the search... and still no traces of the rogue Gyv'Rathi ship. Had the Science Directorate made some grievous error? It wasn't like their ages-old nemesis had made recovering technology from their battered corpse all that easy. Four planetary computational arrays worked day and night just to decrypt what might turn out to be a restaurant's holiday menu. Yes, each victory brought them a little closer to their goal, but still even the smallest setback was eminently frustrating. And the worst part of it was that they could easily travel right past their true objective without ever knowing it. Their limited numbers did not allow for the most efficacious search.

No. The worst would be if the lost Gyv'Rathi ship was already destroyed. They would have no way to know and could possibly spend the rest of their lives on a fruitless search. Well… maybe not their entire lives. Eventually, the attrition of age would reduce the ships' complements down to the point where the ships were no longer viable, and the task force would have to head for home.

But Uxilor did not like that thought. Not at all. He wanted to be home, surrounded by his family, and working his way up the ranks until he achieved true power. Then—and only then—could he challenge for the right of succession, and if he stood victorious from *that*, he would rule the Tovasq Dominion.

He sighed as he closed his eyes. It was a nice dream. A pleasant dream. But it would never come to pass unless he escaped this pointless drudgery.

6

Captain's Day-Cabin, Battle-Carrier *Haven*
En Route to Gateway
22 September 3004, 08:15 GST

Cole accessed his implant and selected the Comms function, instructing it to place a call to Captain Vasquez aboard Babylon Station. Considering he diverted the battlegroup to take the captured Coalition ships and the passenger liners to Gateway, he felt it only fair to warn Vasquez he was on the way.

As soon as he saw the text 'Initiating Call' in his field of view, Cole instructed his implant to switch the call over to main screen in his cabin and use the cabin's audio system. The screen activated and displayed the ship's crest with that same 'Initiating Call' text under it.

Moments later, the screen shifted to the view of Captain Vasquez's office aboard the station, with the man himself front and center in the foreground.

"Greetings, sir. What can Babylon Station do for you today?"

Cole smiled. "I just wanted to let you know that I'm bringing some lost sheep your way."

"Oh? Did some scurvy pirates get past you to destroy a freighter?"

"Of course not," Cole answered with a laugh. "We left the convoy in the Hagen system and came across a running battle in Mu Vega on the way back. We have four passenger liners with disabled engines, one with compromised life support whose passengers are aboard *Haven*, and the other five inside our hyperdrive bubble like we brought the Clanhold from Centauri. It's hard to say right now, since we don't have any scouts out that way, but these people may be all that remains of the free and sovereign Kirkland system."

Vasquez's expression fell. "Kirkland's what... a couple hundred lightyears spinward toward Old Earth? Maybe closer to three hundred?"

"Something like that. I want to say it's a hundred lightyears beyond the Duchy of Musilar."

"Damn... they're really branching out. You think they're heading for the Solars?"

Cole shrugged. "No idea. I have half a mind to ask Srexx if he could maintain a data feed if we parked a stealthed scout frigate off the tail of that Coalition Alpha we saw in Musilar and get a better idea of what they're doing."

"I'm sure he'd jump at the chance to try, but I'm sure that dreadnought is nowhere near Musilar now. We'd have to find it again."

Cole scratched at his chin. "That wouldn't be too hard. Sev is already working on building the home fleets for the Protectorate systems. He could divert the frigate bays at Citadel Station long enough to make a fleet of scout frigates. Hrmmm... this bears further thought. Thanks."

Vasquez chuckled. "Glad I could help. I'll alert the local queen that we'll have a large batch of refugees to interview plus more Coalition ships. I'm not sure how secure this queen is with our agreement, by the way. She seems awfully eager to be useful and help us."

"I'll see about having a chat with her while we're in the system," Cole replied. "Maybe I can do something to put her mind at ease. Thanks for letting me know."

"Of course, sir. Anything else I can do to help?"

Cole turned the question over in his mind a couple times before he shook his head. "No, I don't think so. I mainly wanted you to be aware that we bring you more work."

"Gee… thanks. We'll be ready when you arrive."

"Thanks. Cole out."

ELIZABETH MENDELSON PLACED her tray on the table before she pulled back a chair. Any number of the Kirkland refugees tried to carry the tray for her, and still more seemed angered by her insistence that she was no longer a princess when she declined their service. The simple truth was that she could not see any ways in which Kirkland returned to even a shadow of its former supposed glory.

In looking over her former home's recent years, it seemed apparent to Elizabeth that Kirkland had been in stagnation, if not decline. Kirkland was a stub system one jump off the primary trade route between the Solar Republic and the Aurelian Commonwealth, similar in many respects to Coleson's Beta Magellan. But unlike Beta Magellan, Kirkland did not have an ultra-wealthy sponsor driven with ambition.

Well… the 'driven with ambition' part was up for debate. Her father always talked grand plans to build Kirkland's resurgence, but it seemed like he was always long on talk and short on action. Aside from its population, Elizabeth didn't see what attracted the Coalition to attack the system in the first place. The system did not have any unique or especially valuable resources, and the Coalition had better sources for fuel and reaction mass much closer to 'home.' But she had never been a strategist, especially on a galactic scale, so she quickly concluded that the Coalition leadership saw something in Kirkland she herself did not.

She tucked her napkin onto her lap and collected her utensils, looking at the feast before her with an anticipatory smile. Mister Coleson had certainly been correct about the quality of the food aboard. If the average dining hall delivered food that was on par with the finest fare on the *Princess Kathryn*, what were high-end dining experiences like? It took all her will to maintain a slip of decorum as she dug into her breakfast, and the first bite rewarded her patience and perseverance. Delicious.

As she ate, Elizabeth reflected on those among her immediate circle who acted offended on her behalf that Mister Coleson was not bending over backward to gain her favor. She suspected they were more offended that *they themselves* couldn't elevate their status through proximity to her family, as they had done for longer than she'd been alive. That rung with far more truth than their supposed concern for her station.

"Hello," a voice said, pulling Elizabeth out of her thoughts. She looked up and found the speaker to be a stunning woman with honey blond hair and wearing a *Haven* shipsuit. "You look like you could use a friend; most dining hall tables rarely have only one person sitting at them... unless it's Cole. Would you like some company?"

Elizabeth was just as happy by herself, if she were being honest. She spent her days surrounded by people, and the brief reprieve meals gave her was beyond a blessing. Still, she didn't want to appear rude, especially since she was a guest in what amounted to this woman's home.

"Please, pick a seat," she said, gesturing at the seven available candidates. "I'm Elizabeth Mendelson."

The newcomer chose a seat two chairs around the table from Elizabeth, where she could see the entire dining hall. As soon as she was settled, she gave Elizabeth a warm smile. "It's nice to meet you. I'm Sasha Thyrray."

Elizabeth replied to Sasha's smile with her own. "You mentioned a 'Cole' and how she or he usually ate alone. I've met many people since I came aboard, but I'm not sure I've met this person. Is there a reason they don't have others with them?"

Sasha's smile shifted into something reminiscent of the smile Elizabeth's mother always gave her when she made some social gaff and she should have already known the correct conduct, and she went back over her statement. Well, she hadn't met anyone named 'Cole,' had she? She certainly didn't remember anyone introducing her- or himself as 'Cole.'

"I'm sorry," Sasha said all at once. "I'm so used to everyone knowing that I forget it's usually just among us 'old timers.' You already have met Cole; he greeted you on the flight deck."

Elizabeth's eyes shot wide when she connected the dots. This woman called the wealthiest man in human space 'Cole?'

A chuckle escaped Sasha's lips, and she quickly covered her mouth. "I'm sorry. I'm so sorry. I shouldn't find it amusing. But yes, he's only 'Bartholomew James Coleson' when he has to be. Much prefers 'Cole.'"

Elizabeth cast a cautious glance around the dining hall before turning back to Sasha. "And *everyone* calls him 'Cole?'"

"Well, they would if I let them. I'm the first officer, too, and I insist on a certain amount of discipline aboard. His most ardent supporters tend to shorten Captain to 'Cap,' and it's easier to let that slide than have Cole and I publicly disagreeing in front of the crew." A shadow flitted across Sasha's expression for the briefest moment; it happened so quickly that Elizabeth wondered if she imagined it.

They ate in silence for several moments before Elizabeth worked up the courage to ask, "What's to become of us? I mean, you'd have to ask Captain Villers what his plan was, because all he'd ever say was that we were going somewhere safe. But how can anywhere be safe with the Coalition running around unfettered?"

Sasha's expression conveyed respect, understanding, and no small slice of empathy. "We're taking all of you to Babylon Station. That's in the system we call Gateway. There, people will evaluate your skills and interests and see if we have any openings that match; if we do, we'll extend offers to begin the journey toward becoming a citizen of Beta Magellan. If we don't have any openings that match or for those who prefer to move on, we'll provide transportation to a destination of the person's choice. Freighters with passenger berths and passenger liners dock at Babylon Station every day, so it shouldn't be too diffi-cult to plot an itinerary to deliver someone anywhere in human space."

Elizabeth nodded to show her understanding and went back to her food. After several moments, she said, "Please, forgive me for putting this on you, but may I ask you a question?"

Sasha shrugged. "Sure. I can't promise I'll answer or have the answer you want, but you're welcome to ask me anything."

"Is it wrong that I feel relief that I don't have to be a princess anymore?" Sasha's eyes shot wide, and she set to coughing. "I mean, everyone and their brother keeps trying to shoehorn me into being their princess, the so-called Last Princess of Kirkland... but I never wanted to be a princess in the first place, and on top of that, it seems like lying almost to keep trading on that story. Kirkland has fallen. It's over. Done. Why can't people move on?"

Sasha stopped coughing and took a huge drink of water before she said, "Excuse me for that. Your question caught me by surprise, because I had not yet looked over the list of people we brought aboard. But to answer your question... no, I don't think it's wrong. I used to be a Thyrray of Aurelius. My ancestor signed the colony charter. Now, unlike you, I *wanted* to be a Thyrray of Aurelius and looked forward to my turn leading and guiding the Commonwealth. But like your home, the Commonwealth's time is past, and I doubt it will ever come again. At least not like it was. For the most part, I'm proud of the life I've built with Cole and the Haven Protectorate. I have my family, for which I'm so grateful that Cole has told me to stop thanking him when it comes up. I have my health, and I have my freedom. And for the most part, I'm right where I want to be."

"Why for the most part?"

Sasha held Elizabeth's gaze for several moments before she shook her head. "If you don't mind, I'd rather not discuss that. It's not really germane to the topic."

Elizabeth blinked. "Oh. Okay. I'm sorry; I didn't mean to come across as prying."

"You didn't, I promise. It's just a recent development in my personal life and still something of a sore spot. I'd just rather not discuss it, that's all."

"Totally understand that. I'd rather not discuss trying to force

'Princess of Kirkland' down everyone's throats, but that doesn't stop all the toadies who made their names kissing my family's collective asses down through the years. I at least am more respectful and understanding than Kirkland court toadies. So, any idea when we'll arrive at this Babylon Station?"

Sasha frowned as she took another bite. After swallowing, she replied, "I think the last ETA I saw was something like October 15th. Mu Vega—where we found you—is about seventy-five lightyears from Gateway, and we can't exactly make normal cruising speed and bring along all the ships that we are."

"Wait… we're not using the jump gate network?"

"Nope. Srexx calls it a hyperdrive, because the actual name is too technical for translation… whatever that means. Regardless, we don't have to follow the jump gates for long distance travel, but we choose to do so if we're just hopping one system over. At that point, the jump gates are the better choice."

Elizabeth felt sure her amazement dominated her expression. "Wow. How come that hasn't been distributed throughout the rest of human space? Someone could make a mint off that technology."

"*That* is a very long discussion and one we should probably wait to have until you decide whether or not you'd like to stay with Beta Magellan."

"Oh, I see," even though she didn't, really. Was it proprietary tech maybe? That seemed like the best explanation, but how did they keep it from getting out of their control? Sometimes, it seemed like everything about *Haven* and its people simply created more questions with every answer.

Sasha finished her breakfast and collected her dishes and utensils. "Now, please, don't think I'm ducking out on you, but I need to get to the bridge. I'm taking Beta Shift in a little over thirty minutes."

Elizabeth nodded and did her best at a permissive gesture. "Thank you for the conversation. I enjoyed the company."

"If you or your people need anything, just call the bridge and ask to speak to the officer of the deck," and with that, Sasha disappeared into the sea of people, leaving Elizabeth to her thoughts.

7

B abylon Station
Gateway
18 October 3004, 11:22 GST

Elizabeth stepped off the shuttle from *Haven* and took in her new surroundings. She felt nervous, unsettled. She *knew* the battle-carrier was not home and would not be home, but she had become emotionally connected to the peace it afforded her during the trip from Mu Vega to Gateway. While aboard *Haven*, she could get away with being Elizabeth. Not Princess Elizabeth, and absolutely not Queen Elizabeth. Just Elizabeth. Lizzie if she ever met that special someone; she'd loved the sound of that since she was little, but her mother went through three shades of red in her distress over the idea of shortening a fine name of such regal pedigree.

If she were being totally honest, a part of her nerves came from the fact that she'd asked—okay… maybe begged—a separate ride over to the station than the rest of the refugees. Yes, she wanted to know they were taken care of. Yes, she wanted them to have what they needed. But she also wanted them to get used to the idea of living without a royal family. Because she didn't want to live out her life like that, let alone have such a responsibility over others. Even if she'd been the type to thrive in that role, it still seemed hypocritical in the extreme to style herself a princess—or stars forbid a queen—when she had nothing to be princess or queen over.

"Elizabeth?"

She turned at the sound of her name and found herself facing a woman about her age… maybe a little older. "Yes?"

"Hi, I'm Victoria Rainier. Cole sent word that you asked him to slip you aboard Babylon Station, and he asked if I could help you get settled."

Elizabeth smiled. "Thank you. That was very kind of him."

Victoria replied with a slight smile. "I haven't been here all that long, but I think Cole knows what it's like to want something else but be locked in a role he ultimately built for himself."

"Someone's taking care of the Kirkland people, yes? Seeing to their needs?"

"Oh, yes; we're rather proficient at caring for refugees at this point," Victoria answered. "I was part of the last large group to arrive. Now, if you're ready, I've arranged a refugee orientation for you that won't take you through the normal places where you might run into any of your people."

Elizabeth felt her cheeks heat in a blush. "Cole told you?"

"Yes, but he wouldn't have needed to. I recognize you from a trade summit several years ago that my father hosted at Musilar."

"Is it bad that I just want to put the past behind me and start fresh?"

Victoria shook her head as she led Elizabeth away from the concourse and into corridors. "Not at all. My father and I haven't given up on all the people in the former duchy, but at the same time, there's little we can do. Cole is still building up his forces, and he has too many commitments right now to engage in a campaign to roll back the Coalition. But soon, he will."

"So, I have another question I'm a little ashamed to ask," Elizabeth said.

"Please, don't feel ashamed. Whatever it is, I guarantee you I've heard it before."

Elizabeth took a breath. Then, a second. "I'd like to change my name. Cole told me that part of the reception procedure is to record a person's name and biometrics. I can't do anything about my biometrics, but I'd like to put the Mendelsons and their legacy behind me."

"See? That wasn't so bad, was it? And that won't be a problem. We have actually encountered something like this before. So, we run two different databases. One is the refugee database that is publicly searchable, with the goal of finding loved ones and such; yes, there is the opportunity for abuse, but we try to give only general information beyond what's necessary for someone to confirm another's identity. The other database is our citizen database that is not publicly searchable and has significant controls in place to ensure only authorized requests may search the system; from what I understand, Srexx oversees the security of *that* database personally. What we'll do is simply not record your data in the refugee database; I'm sure someone will take issue with that, but that's on them. Have you decided on a name?"

"Elizabeth Cavanaugh. My great-great-grandmother had that name, and I've always liked it."

Victoria smiled. "That's perfect. It's always better to have a personal connection to a new identity."

COLE SAW how Captain Vasquez fought the urge to snap to attention as he entered the man's office. The station commander managed to stop his reflex, so Cole didn't feel the need to make an issue of it.

"Captain," Cole said, extending his hand as they met, "how goes the refugee processing?"

Vasquez gave him a respectable handshake and gestured to some seating. "It's going well. As is always the case, a certain percentage simply is not compatible with our goals and interests... for a myriad of reasons. We've already split them across freighters due to leave soon, and they'll be off the station within a couple hours or so. Your special refugee has been processed and passed the evaluation for citizenship with flying colors."

Cole chuckled and shook his head. "She's not *my* refugee. I just appreciate her situation. Carrying a legacy isn't for everyone."

The hatch opened behind them, and Cole turned. Victoria Rainier led Elizabeth into the room, and both Cole and Vasquez stood to greet them.

"Cole, it is my pleasure to introduce to you Elizabeth Cavanaugh," Victoria said, giving a small flourish to indicate Elizabeth.

"It's nice to meet you, Ms. Cavanaugh," Cole said, a smile tugging at his lips. "I trust you find our humble station to your liking."

Elizabeth seemed in the midst of a rear-guard action against her own mirth; the corners of her mouth kept trying to quirk upward as if to smile. "Why, thank you, good sir. I have to say that your 'humble station' as you put it is far and away the most incredible sight I have ever beheld."

"Have you given any thought to where you'll go next?" Cole asked.

"Well, Victoria tells me I have qualified for Beta Magellan citizenship if I want it. I'm not quite sure *how*, but I'm happy to take her word for it. Did you pull some strings for me?"

Cole was quick to shake his head. "Oh, no. I pull strings for no one when it comes to the refugee assessment. In our earliest days, when we were just *Haven*, Sasha and Talia had prices on their heads from the Provisional Parliament of the Aurelian Commonwealth, and I had to be sure no one who came aboard *Haven* did so for nefarious purposes. Now, it's just become something of an accepted thing. I've tried to do away with it a couple times, but the people were quick to beg me not to. It seems they like knowing their next-door neighbor wants to be there as much as they do... and for basically the same reason."

Elizabeth's expression turned curious. "How do you do it? Or is that a state secret?"

"No, it's not a state secret, not really. Did Victoria sit and chat with you for a while after introducing you to some nice non-humans that you may never have encountered before?"

"Oh, yes! I met my first Ghrexel *and* my first Kiksalik. They were so nice. The Ghrexel had a simply adorable color pattern in her fur."

Cole nodded along as Elizabeth recounted the experience. When she ended, his expression dimmed a bit, and he said, "The Kiksaliks are telepaths. They can read our minds like we read books or datascreens."

Elizabeth gaped. "What? *That* was my refugee assessment? But... but we didn't talk about anything! Well, nothing serious. The Ghrexel was an artist who was learning human knitting and weaving for techniques to meld into her style. We never discussed anything about whether I would ever consider betraying Beta Magellan or anything like that."

"Of course not," Cole replied with a smile. "You would've been tense if you had gone into the conversation knowing why you were having it, and I've been told that kind of tension can make the whole experience unpleasant."

"I *know* I'll regret asking this, but how do you know?"

Cole sighed. "When I went to Centauri to claim my inheritance, someone attempted to kill me within—I think maybe—four hours of setting foot on the station my family built. A dear friend jumped into the line of fire and took the hit for me, and when we finally found the shooter, he was rather uncooperative. By the time the Kiksaliks finished with him, he bled out of both nostrils *and* both ears."

Elizabeth shook herself. She wasn't quite sure how to process all that. First, that someone would try to kill someone who seemed like a decent person, and two, that the nice insectoid she met could've chosen to hurt her as he or she—maybe it?—rummaged through her mind.

One more reason she wasn't about to let anyone talk her into trying for the Captain of *Haven*. Aside from all that, Cole was simply too high-profile. She would never be able to maintain her longed-for obscurity if she set her cap for him. Plus, it would open him up to any schemers from her family's court who managed to pass the refugee exam. Frankly, after learning what it was, she doubted any would... but better safe than sorry.

"Have you given any thought what you'd like to do now?" Cole asked.

"Not really, no. I've always loved animals, but I doubt Beta Magellan or any of its holdings has much call for a veterinarian."

Cole grinned. "You might be surprised. Victoria, do you mind showing her the skills and aptitude assessment?"

"Not at all, Cole. It was our next stop."

Elizabeth fought the urge to blush. She didn't like how he made her feel shy and borderline embarrassed. Her mother would be aghast if she knew. "Well, I don't want to keep you. I simply asked Victoria if I could thank you in person for this wonderful chance at a fresh start."

"You're very welcome, Elizabeth. Take care of yourself, and remember... have fun."

Elizabeth replied with a weak smile and a few short nods before she and Victoria left the office.

Cole watched them leave and sighed over a path not taken. Some days, he really wished he *had* bought that planet and disappeared. Then, his other reason for visiting Vasquez returned to his mind, and he withdrew a small box from his pocket. The box held a jewelry box that might have contained an engagement ring, and he no longer wanted it taunting him on *Haven*.

"When's the next courier to Beta Magellan?" Cole asked.

Vasquez frowned. "Uhm... a couple hours, I think. Not more than three. Why?"

Cole tossed him the box that—at its very heart—held a ring worth more than some planets' gross domestic product. "See that makes it to my apartment on Citadel Station or my house down on Four, please."

Vasquez was a little awkward in his catch, but the box didn't bounce off the desk or the decking. "Does it need any special handling?"

"No," Cole answered. "I'm just tired of carrying it around *Haven* with me."

If Vasquez held any suspicions as to the box's contents, he did not voice or indicate them in any way. He simply nodded. "I'll see to it, sir."

"Thank you," Cole replied. "Is there any other noteworthy news?"

"No. Everything's been pretty much by the numbers here."

Cole pushed himself to his feet. "Well then, I guess that means my work here is done. Call me if you need me."

Vasquez nodded and stepped around the desk as he said, "Naturally, sir."

They turned, and Vasquez walked with Cole to the shuttle that would take him back to *Haven*.

8

En Route to Spark
    Battle-Carrier *Haven*
22 October 3004, 18:27 GST

People packed *Chromosphere* to the bulkheads that night. Which was both good and bad. Good, in that there was so much background noise someone would've had to stand at a table to eavesdrop. Bad, in that anyone trying to talk almost had to shout. Fortunately, the proprietor made allowances for nights like these. During the space's renovation, he set aside a section for privacy booths. When active, the serving staff had to press a key notifying the occupants of his or her presence and request permission to enter.

Garrett kept a standing reservation for one of the privacy booths. They normally couldn't be reserved, operating instead on a first-come first-served basis, but Garrett tended to treat the booth like his office. It wasn't long before word got around that the guy who always sat in the first privacy booth was the captain's spymaster, and they forgave him for keeping the booth busy. Well, that and no one wanted to cross him. There were *stories*.

That particular evening, Garrett enjoyed his meal in the company of none other than Red. It had been a little while since they sat around chatting, and Garrett had invited him to dinner to correct that unfortunate circumstance.

"So, congratulations on the promotion," Garrett remarked. "I'm glad Cole took Mazzi up on her recommendation when she transferred to the cruiser."

Red finished his swallow and saluted Garrett with the glass. "Thank you. I was pleased to learn that Mazzi felt so highly of me that she recommended me for both Operations Officer *and* Alpha Shift Weapons Officer. A few stray comments led me to believe they're supposed to be separate positions, but Mazzi didn't want to leave the weapons station. I can't say I'd want to, either. There's something rather thrilling about having such firepower at the touch of one's fingers."

Garrett chuckled. "I'm sure. I've always preferred nimble and fast, myself. If I'm going to be traveling alone, anyway. Ships like this are fine if you're a passenger or not attached to the ship's company, but there's a reason I never joined any of the navies."

"Cole does a good job of keeping things as loose as possible aboard," Red replied. "This is about as un-military as I've ever seen."

"Say... have you heard much around the ship about the current situation between Cole and Sasha?"

Red shook his head to answer 'no.' "Not really. Not beyond the rumors flying about what started it, and most of those tell a fairly accurate rendition of what happened. So, I haven't bothered to correct anyone."

"Ah, good. So, it isn't affecting morale?"

Red frowned for a moment before answering, "No, I don't think so. Several of the ladies aboard wish they had a shot at Cole if he has suddenly become available, but by and large, most people feel bad for them. After all, they seemed happy together."

Garrett shrugged. "Just between you and me, I've been wondering when the wheels would come off the wagon. At their cores, they have a lot of similar desires and intents... but how they pursue those goals are wildly different. Cole spent most of his formative adult years masquerading as Jax Theedlow, and that colored him. How much, I'm sure we'll never know. In many ways, he probably would've been happy to live out his days as a freighter pilot, and if he hadn't found this ship *and* survived the Pyllesc system, he could've used the Jax Theedlow identity to purchase a freighter and run clean cargo. But events didn't take him that way."

"I—for one—am glad they didn't," Red countered. "There's no telling where either one of us would be now, if Cole hadn't come to Iota Ceti."

"You do have a point. We were in kinda dire straits there. So, it's really none of our business either way, but what do you think about Cole dating Scarlett? They have some chemistry, and it might work."

Red disagreed. "I don't really see that. Managing Baldur and Midas might have evened her out a little, but Scarlett is—and always will be —chaotic at heart. She enjoys thrills and excitement. I'm not sure that's someone you want at the right hand of the wealthiest-known human. And you're also correct in that it isn't any of our business beyond there being an heir in case something happens. *But...* unless the Trust is written to require it, the heir doesn't have to be Cole's blood descendant, just the person Cole chooses in front of witnesses. Yes, granted, everyone would prefer the heir to be Cole's child raised by him; it increases the odds you'll inherit a similar authority figure to Cole. I don't think we'll have to worry about personality drift until Cole's grandchild or possibly great-grandchild. At that point, they will not have had access to Cole as part of their education. *That* is when we will start seeing Beta Magellan drift away from Cole's core values... unless something is done to prevent it."

"All good points," Garrett remarked as the notification of a server requesting access pinged. Garrett granted access, and they received their food and refills for their drinks.

The server slipped back out, and the privacy screen reactivated while Garrett and Red dug into their food.

~

ELIZABETH FOLLOWED Victoria to the liner that would take her to Citadel Station in Beta Magellan. She was not the only passenger, but none of the other passengers were Kirkland refugees. Victoria and the other refugee staff gave her a head start to get lost among the population of Beta Magellan before any of 'her' people who chose Beta Magellan arrived there.

If she were being honest with herself, she was more than a little nervous. She had no real salable skills beyond smiling to a crowd, waving, and reading prepared speeches… but Victoria assured her that would not be a problem. She had already arranged for a sponsor family to meet her when the liner docked, which was a custom in Beta Magellan and its territories. The sponsor family would help her wend her way through the nuances of establishing herself in Beta Magellan.

"Are you ready to go?" Victoria asked as they arrived at the hatch where passengers already boarded the *Star of Hope*.

Elizabeth took a breath and exhaled it as a sigh. "I'm not sure, honestly, but if I don't go, I never will be. Self-determination is something of a new world for me, and I'm not quite sure how to go about it."

Victoria replied with a patient smile. "I've been where you are, kind of anyway. Take it a day at a time, and don't expect everything to happen at once."

"I'll work on remembering that," Elizabeth said, adding an encouraging nod. She hoped it was encouraging, anyway.

"You have my comms code, and I expect you to use it. And don't you ever think sending me a message is a bother. Okay?"

Elizabeth smiled and nodded once more. "I'll remember that. Thanks. I never imagined charting my own course would be so exhilarating and terrifying… all at the same time.

Victoria pulled her into a friendly hug. "One day, you'll wake up and wonder how you've ever done anything else. Just remember… be patient and give it time. Okay… they just posted last call for passengers. Take care of yourself, Lizzy."

Elizabeth beamed as she waved and led her small luggage through the hatch.

~

Victoria watched Elizabeth board the liner that would take her to her future… whatever she decided that would be. In her heart of hearts, she *knew* Elizabeth would be okay, but she still remembered the underlying anxiety of 'what do I do now' when she first arrived on Babylon Station. At least, she had people looking up to her and relying on her. Elizabeth could've had that, too… if she had wanted it.

But Victoria also understood the desire to live the life *she* chose. That had been a tantalizing 'what if' in the back of her mind since her adolescence. Maybe one day… when the refugees coming to Gateway tapered off or she no longer enjoyed helping them… she'd investigate self-determination a little more. But for right now, she was where she felt the most useful.

The hatch to *Star of Hope* sealed, and moments later the hatch tell-tales indicated that no ship was docked in that bay. Victoria accessed her implant and fired off a quick text to Cole, saying that she had seen Elizabeth safely to a liner bound for Citadel Station without any Kirk-landers aboard.

As she left the docking area, a thought brought a slight smile to her expression. She still remembered the wide-eyed, mind-boggled expressions Elizabeth's sponsor family developed when Victoria passed them access to and control of the modest stipend Cole had left to get Elizabeth established in new life. Someone should probably have a quiet word with Cole that 'modest' in numerical form didn't usually have so many zeroes.

~

The most recent contact report from the Revtamat sensors was not encouraging. Despite traveling anti-spinward at eighty percent on the hyperdrive, the contact's bearing relative to *Haven* continued to edge toward 'dead ahead.' The bearing to the contact was approximately three-hundred fifteen degrees, using the human measurements.

Srexx had still not found a time he felt appropriate to discuss the matter with Cole, and the more time that passed, the more he evaluated that he would just have to interrupt Cole or schedule a time to converse. After all, the odds of the contact existing at all being significant were rather high, based on his calculations.

And if the sensors were calibrated properly—by no means a sure thing—the signal strength of the contact seemed to be increasing at a slow but measurable rate. Which would only happen if the range to the contact was decreasing. No. Srexx could *not* let this matter lie for much longer.

But should he tell Cole before Spark or after? That question required further analysis.

9

Bridge, Battle-Carrier *Haven*
    Spark System
30 October 3004, 07:37 GST

Cole leaned back against the command chair as the battlegroup decelerated on approach to the system's sole inhabited planet. The tactical plot showed a system awash with traffic, both small craft like shuttles and miner capsules and also larger civilian vessels like freighters and ore haulers. It seemed like the system was rebounding well from its time as a subjugated member of the Coalition.

According to Garrett, there was more than sufficient evidence to put the Minister of Trade on a prison planet for the rest of his life. The only question was how to proceed. Should they hand over everything to the local authorities and trust them to handle it? Or should it be part of Beta Magellan's remit within the Haven Protectorate?

On ancient Earth, the federal governments often only concerned themselves—on paper, anyway—with crimes that crossed state or province lines and/or affected interstate or inter-province commerce. Even though the Protectorate was not strictly a federal system, should Beta Magellan's role be that of a federal government? Only concern itself with crimes that crossed system boundaries or affected interstellar commerce? The piracy case that brought them to the system certainly did that, but at the same time, the Protectorate Treaty also obligated Beta Magellan to system defense for its members.

The whole situation was a thorny problem, and the more Cole delved into it, the less enthused he was that he'd allowed the member systems to draw himself and Beta Magellan into it.

"Incoming challenge, Cap," Jenkins at Comms announced. "Captain Luzader of the *Agamemnon* has ordered us to identify ourselves or heave to."

Cole discarded the first three responses that flitted through his mind. After all, there was *zero* chance that the cruiser-led task force serving as a system defense force didn't recognize *Haven* and her battlegroup. The only thing that seemed more absurd to Cole's mind was a Chihuahua challenging a Doberman… or perhaps a Mastiff.

"I am *very* tempted to ask you to tell Captain Luzader to make us, Jenkins. He has one cruiser, twelve destroyers, and twenty-four frigates to throw against our battlegroup." Cole paused for a moment. "You know… on second thought, send this word for word. Ready?"

"Ready, Cap."

"Cole would like to know just what you'd do if you caught us, Captain," Cole dictated.

Jenkins tapped at his console for a few moments before reporting, "And… sent, Cap."

Not even a full minute later, the console chirped, and Jenkins barked a laugh. Then, he said, "Captain Luzader says he'd probably run like hell, Cap, and welcomes you to Spark."

Cole smiled. "Kindly thank him for his welcome, Jenkins. Helm, maintain course and deceleration for Spark V."

THE BATTLEGROUP SLID into orbit around the fifth planet in the Spark system without any fanfare or challenge. Cole halfway expected a reaction of some sort to their arrival, but despite giving them a whole thirty minutes, nothing happened. Of course, there was always the chance that the identities of the ships now trailing the planet's orbital station hadn't reached the planetary government yet, and it was also possible that no one cared.

"Comms, send word to the planetary governor that I would appreciate a few minutes of his time. A holo-call is fine; there's no reason to come down to the planet," Cole said after an extra fifteen minutes of no reaction.

Moments later, the spacer at Comms reported, "An aide in the planetary governor's office says that he is booked through next month, sir."

Cole nodded. "I see. Something tells me that aide just lost his or her job, but no matter. We'll proceed with Plan B. Srexx, have you located the Minister of Trade as yet?"

The overhead speakers chirped and broadcast Srexx's voice, "Yes, Cole. The Minister of Trade is currently meeting with the planetary governor, along with several other ministers."

"Oh, my... this will get a bit messy. Marine Ops, my compliments to Colonel Devereaux if you please; ask her if she is ready to execute the search and arrest warrants on the Minister of Trade."

A few seconds later, the spacer replied, "Sir, she says that she and the CAG are ready to go at your order."

"Sound battle stations and alert the carrier group to prepare for orbital overwatch," Cole said, "and Marine Ops, please pass one word to Colonel Devereaux: go."

As one squadron of fighters and an assault shuttle launched, the ships that made up the battlegroup shifted position to accommodate any overwatch duties that might be required. Soon, additional squadrons of fighters accompanied the assault shuttles that left *Haven*. The fledgling Haven Protectorate Judiciary issued several search and seizure warrants on Spark's Minister of Trade in the wake of the sheer overwhelming mass of evidence gathered from the captured pirate ships.

It seemed the launching of five assault shuttles escorted by a squadron of fighters served as sufficient provocation to grab the attention of local authorities.

"Cap," Jenkins at Comms reported, "we're being challenged by

Spark Planetary Defense. They are ordering us to identify ourselves and recall our small craft, or they will open fire."

Cole chuckled. "Inform them that we are executing search and seizure warrants authorized by the Haven Protectorate Judiciary and that any attempt to interfere will be met with appropriate levels of force... up to and including lethal. Feel free to include copies of the warrants, and if that doesn't sort the issue, send them a link to the video of the Caledonia bombardment."

"Aye, Cap."

"Srexx, are you working on your part in this?" Cole asked.

The overhead speakers chirped and broadcast Srexx's voice. "Of course, Cole. I have been since we entered the system. I would not have been able to do so until we arrived in orbit, had we not installed quantum comms units in the station and at various points in the planet's datanet."

"Thanks, Srexx," Cole replied.

"Of course, Cole."

The overhead speakers chirped once more, signaling the comms channel closed.

Silence extended for several minutes while the search and seizure teams approached their assigned locations. The marine staffing the Marine Ops station reported each team's arrival as it happened, and Cole felt they were making progress toward a successful, no-excitement resolution.

But he was wrong...

"Cap, we have a runner," Haskell at Sensors announced. "A ship just left the planet with the Minister of Trade aboard. It launched from the planetary governor's private spaceport, and its current course points toward the Emerald jump gate."

"Jenkins, send a destroyer and three frigates on intercept orders. Srexx, expand your search to include the planetary governor. I didn't think he was implicated in this at all."

Jenkins replied, "Aye, Cap."

"Yes, Cole," Srexx responded.

A few more minutes passed while Cole waited for word and

considered the situation. It seemed like everyone was complying with the warrants without any significant resistance. Or at least without resistance that required an orbital overwatch.

"Red, re-work the battlegroup's deployment from an orbital over-watch to full planetary coverage in case we have any more runners. I'd rather we not have to chase them halfway into the outer system if we don't have to. Transmit the new formation orders to TacNet as soon as you have them."

The massive Igthon at the weapons station nodded. "Aye, Cap."

Cole watched the plot as the battlegroup re-position over the next twenty minutes. The longer he sat there, the more he couldn't shake the feeling that this was going too well.

"Cap," Jenkins said, "the captain of the fast packet carrying the Minister of Trade is refusing to heave to and prepare to be boarded. He claims to have diplomatic immunity as the planetary governor's personal transport."

Cole chuckled again. "Please tell me we have that refusal recorded."

"We do, Cap." Cole heard the smile in Jenkins's voice without needing to swivel to face him.

"Send a message to Beta Magellan to double-check that—one—members of the Protectorate do *not* have diplomatic immunity from the Protectorate Judiciary and—two—to request search and seizure warrants on the planetary governor for aiding and abetting the trade minister's flight from justice. Be sure to flag that as immediate prior-ity, too."

A few moments later, Jenkins reported, "Sent, Cap."

"Good. Now, hail that fast packet. I want to speak to the captain and be sure the destroyer and frigates on-site can hear but not interrupt."

Moments later, Jenkins responded, "I have the captain."

"Put him on the main screen."

The screen at the front of the bridge activated to display a tight view of a slightly pudgy man approaching the upper end of middle age. His complexion looked flushed, whether with health concerns or anger was difficult to say.

"Hello," Cole said as he leaned back against the command chair, "I am Bartholomew James Coleson, commanding the *Haven* battlegroup. We came to Spark to execute search and seizure warrants against the man you're transporting aboard your ship. Now, I understand you're refusing to heave to on the basis that you claim diplomatic immunity. I have forwarded this matter to the Haven Protectorate Judiciary in Beta Magellan for immediate review, and I expect an answer shortly. In the interests of calm and respectful relations, I ask that you null your drives and hold position until we get a response."

The longer Cole spoke, the redder the captain became. "How dare you! I will do no such thing! I am under direct command of the planetary governor of Spark, and I do not recognize your authority to order me to have a good day, let alone heave to and prepare to be boarded."

"Very well," Cole replied. "I'm afraid you leave me no choice, then. Red, order the task group assigned to capture that ship to disable its engines and return it to Spark. Goodbye, Captain; we'll see you when you return to the planet. *Haven* out."

The last image displayed on the screen before it deactivated was the captain's eyes going wide as his jaw dropped.

Twenty minutes later, the Comms console chirped, and Jenkins said, "Cap, response from Beta Magellan. The Judiciary says Protectorate Members *do not* enjoy diplomatic immunity from the Protectorate Judiciary under the terms of the treaty, and they sent along search and seizure warrants on the planetary governor as well."

"Thank you, Jenkins. Please, transmit those warrants to the teams already on-planet and the Judiciary's findings to the captain being towed home."

Jenkins was quick to reply, "You got it, Cap."

Part of Cole didn't enjoy sitting in the command chair on *Haven*'s bridge while his people were on the planet below. That part very much wanted to be leading one of the teams himself as the Lone Marine, but given his position in the hierarchy of things—that is, the top of the pyramid—he understood why he should not be the point of the spear, not matter how much he wanted it.

The task group returned to take up the positions in the orbital coverage, one of the destroyers towing the disabled—and now captured—ship. That particular class of ship was very similar to the *Courageous Sloth* he had co-piloted when he first donned the Jax Theedlow persona; designed for runs delivering high-value and low-volume cargo as quickly as possible, it was little more than a personnel shuttle welded onto a frame with destroyer engines. With its almost-obscene mass-to-thrust ratio, 'conventional' ships would've had a difficult time catching it, if they could at all. Fortunately, Cole's ships were nowhere close to what passed for 'conventional' outside Beta Magellan's sphere of influence.

"Cap, the search and seizure teams are returning," Jenkins announced. "They report the planetary governor and several members of the planetary defense force in custody, in addition to all the physical evidence collected."

Cole shook his head and fought the urge to chuckle. "I'm guessing the governor's security detail decided to duke it out with our marines?"

"That's what the report suggests, Cap... even after the team presented the warrant for the governor's seizure for questioning."

The old, familiar twitch between his shoulder blades returned, and Cole fought the urge to sigh. "I'm going to have to do another press conference, aren't I?"

"Probably, Cap. Planetary media is already going ape over the 'apparent abduction' of their 'stalwart and upstanding governor.'"

"If he were so stalwart and upstanding, he wouldn't have allowed the Trade Minister to use his personal transport," Cole replied, almost muttered. "Fine. Let's get an accurate picture of what's happening here, in terms of the convoy piracy, and I'll do the Centauri thing again."

10

November 3004

Sub-Legate Uxilor eyed the system plot as his task force cruised into the latest system of their search. This system seemed to be the most developed of all the primitive systems they had encountered thus far. There was certainly a much more massive space presence than any of the previous systems possessed. In fact, the sensors crew already identified six ships larger than his own flagship.

While matching the contours of the Gyv'Rathi battle-carriers, his flagship did *not* in fact possess a flight deck or hangar decks for small craft. It possessed the standard shuttle bays for personnel or cargo transfers, but the Tovasq Dominion did not harbor the same mystique —or perhaps, admiration—for small craft and carriers that their ancient nemesis had.

Focusing once more on the data-codes of the six massive ships—at least in terms of their associates—Uxilor felt a surge of anticipation for the first time since arriving in this accursed backwater of a galactic region. Perhaps the six of these ships would at last present his task force a proper challenge.

But that challenge would have to wait. The periodic readiness reports awaited his approval, and if he did not review and approve—

or annotate—them within the time allotted by the Space Directorate, it would be one item they could use against him at his next promotion review.

The last information his eyes found before he switched off the system plot was the name the primitives gave this star system, and it was just as absurd as everything else about them.

They called it Aurelius.

~

RECITAL HALL, Recreation Deck
Battle-Carrier *Haven*
Orbiting Spark V, Spark System
7 November 3o04

The discussion among the assembled journalists filled the hall with the noise that only a large group of people talking at normal volume can create. Most of them shuttled up from the planet earlier that morning, while several had arrived in the system once word spread that Cole had arrested the planetary governor and trade minister. They all faced the small stage, where a podium stood.

When Cole stepped into view on the stage and crossed to the podium, the entire hall was silent—except for his footfalls—by the time he rested his hands on the lectern. They were so focused on him that they didn't even notice the spacers spreading out through the crowd handing each a data crystal.

"Good day," Cole began, "we are here today to discuss the actions I have ordered since arriving in this system a little over a week ago. They are not capricious or tyrannical as the planetary governor's partisans keep asserting. In fact, they are rooted in Haven Protectorate law. All actions I have ordered have been backed by warrants for search and seizure by the Haven Protectorate Judiciary, which we included among data on the crystals.

"Now, these actions are the result of the rash of convoy piracy that has plagued convoys leaving Spark over the past few months. The *Haven* battlegroup accompanied the most recent convoy under full stealth and without advising any ships in the convoy we did so. This led to capturing twenty corvettes that attacked the convoy but tried to flee when faced with superior technology. Needless to say, they were unsuccessful."

Over the next several minutes, Cole continued to summarize the events that led him to Spark, and the events of the search and seizure operations authorized by the Protectorate Judiciary's warrants. Cole held them spellbound as he walked through the evidence on the data crystals. And at last, he reached the true news of his presentation.

"At approximately 18:23 GST yesterday, the planetary governor confessed to working with the trade minister not only to enrich himself and their associates in the scheme but also undermine the Haven Protectorate and my personal integrity under claims that I 'obviously could not uphold Beta Magellan's promises of protection in the Protectorate Charter.' I respectfully submit to you and anyone viewing this conference that such is not the case. Now, I will take questions."

Over the next two hours, Cole fielded question after question from the journalists. Even when those representing partisans of the planetary governor attempted to obfuscate the issues, he stood firm and implacable against their onslaught. When the questions devolved to little more than those partisan representatives trying to bait Cole, he thanked them for their time and reminded them of their contractual agreement to broadcast his statement in full before leaving the hall.

Cole found Garrett waiting for him when he exited the recital hall's backstage hatch. He smiled as his old friend fell into step at his side.

"I thought you might enjoy knowing that we've located five more conspirators in the convoy piracy scheme. We've detailed our evidence to the Judiciary back home and merely await the almost-assured search and seizure warrants."

Cole felt like wincing. "Ouch. What do those bring the count to?"

"Seventeen, so far, and we're only flagging those we have concrete evidence of intentional willful compliance. If we can prove beyond a reasonable doubt that someone was an unwitting pawn or similar, we monitor them to ensure our analysis isn't wrong but otherwise leave them alone. Well... my investigations section monitors them; stars only know what Srexx does."

Now, Cole laughed. "Srexx probably knows their entire lives thus far backward, forward, and sideways with total data continuity for good measure. I'm still trying to teach him the concept of privacy."

"You haven't managed it yet," Garrett countered. "He gave us tera-crystals' worth of data around the time we made orbit, and our warrants at the time covered less than half of it."

"And the warrants we have now or expect to have soon?"

Garrett grunted. "Half to two-thirds, at best. He's going through the planetary datanet like an addict chasing his next fix, and I'm pretty sure he's giving us only the data that pertains to our investigations."

"Do you want him to give you all of it?"

"Not really," Garrett replied. "Not right now, at least. It would just serve to muddy the waters. He knows what we want, and he gives any data even tangentially related to the convoy piracy. Eventually, the intelligence section may find the rest of it useful, but the investigation section doesn't need it."

Cole nodded as they turned into a transit shaft. "How bad is it?"

"Like I said, we've only identified seventeen willful conspirators in the scheme thus far, and we went a few hours without identifying Numbers Sixteen and Seventeen. Unless Srexx comes across some-thing new we haven't seen even hints of, I think these seventeen are it. On a planet with a population close to a billion sapients, seventeen isn't even a rounding error. Still, they were all highly placed in the planetary government or traffic control or similar roles, so if you look at it from that aspect... yeah... it was pretty bad."

"I regret that for the people of Spark," Cole said as they stepped out of the transit shaft on Deck Three, and Cole led them toward his day-cabin. "They don't deserve the turmoil or upheaval this will create. The planetary governor and... what... ten ministers? That's a huge chunk of their executive branch right there. They're going to be a little bit recovering from this, unless the lieutenant governor is truly prepared to assume overall authority at a moment's notice. And how many actually are?"

Garrett countered, "Spark's lieutenant governor seems to be rather on the ball. She has stepped up and appointed people to fill the vacant ministry positions and is already moving on a series of programs to support the families of the convoy personnel who were lost during the piracy. I'm surprised more people didn't clue into how the former governor wasn't all that moved by the loss of those convoys."

"Yeah," Cole agreed. "I would've thought *that* would've been a serious indication that something wasn't quite right."

They turned the corner to enter one of the two main corridors that ran the length of the ship and found Sasha standing at the hatch to Cole's day-cabin, pressing the hatch chime control like mad.

"I don't think I'm home," Cole said, raising his voice enough to carry the distance to Sasha.

Sasha jerked her head around, and some of the tension left her shoulders when she saw Cole and Garrett. She hurried to meet them.

"I'm glad you're here, too, Garrett." Sasha lifted a small data crystal. "I have something both of you need to see."

Cole fought the urge to sigh. When he saw her at the hatch to his cabin, he had allowed himself to hope she was there for personal reasons. Not to make a play on words of it, but it was sometimes a little awkward making sure that their interactions didn't *become* awkward lately. They usually restricted themselves to ship's business only, with no mention of their dating or personal relationship that had seemed so vibrant and strong just a few weeks before.

"Cabin, office, or briefing room?" Cole asked.

Sasha looked off to the side as she worked her lower lip between her teeth for a few moments. She soon asked, "Briefing room please?"

Cole's response was his about-face and return to the briefing room's hatch which was just back around the corner. He didn't wait to see if they followed... which they did. The room's systems activated when Cole stepped through the hatch, and Sasha went straight to the data controls to drop the data crystal into the reader niche. By the time she did that and found a seat for herself, Cole and Garrett sat in their customary seats at either end of the table.

The holo-display activated and showed the frozen image of what appeared to be an INN newscast. Moments later, the recording began.

"Thank you for tuning into this breaking news. I am Sergio Vansantz. On the first of September, a task force of unknown vessels numbering twenty ships in total arrived in the Aurelius system in a manner very similar to that of Beta Magellan's ships. As you will see from the accompanying footage, however, these were *not* Beta Magellan ships. Over the course of two days, this task force of twenty ships engaged and obliterated all space-going shipping in the system, and when the planetary defenses fired on a few of the smaller ships that strayed too close, the task force responded by delivering a brutal bombardment across the entire planet. At this time, we do not have a firm count on casualties or wounded, though we expect both numbers to be very high. From what we are able to determine, it is possible Aurelius—the planet—has been reduced to the Information Age if not pre-Industrial. We have no firm information on the location of this mysterious task force, and the ISA has issued a Yellow advisory urging all vessels to avoid the area at all costs."

Sergio paused for a second, taking a deep breath, before he continued. "We must also report that INN has lost several of its own to this tragedy. A news ship broadcast much of the one-sided conflict live until the invaders finally paid attention to them. Shortly after the start of the bombardment, the invaders destroyed our news ship, killing the twelve people aboard. Further details on this will be forthcoming once we have notified the families of these intrepid journalists; without their sacrifice, we would not know of the threat looming before us. We will now share selected clips of the news ship's two-and-a-half-day broadcast, and we advise you that parts of the following footage may not be suitable for younger viewers. The entire broadcast is available on our site on the galactic datanet."

Cole sat through the accompanying footage in silence, and the more he watched, the more it reminded him of how Coalition ships fared against *Haven* and its battlegroup. Whoever these 'invaders' were, they tore through the Coalition ships in Aurelius like they weren't even there. The six dreadnoughts—including the Coalition Alpha—presented at least a little challenge, but the unknown task force didn't even lose any small ships before the last dreadnought fell silent. By the end of the footage, a cold shiver ran up and down Cole's spine like it participated in some kind of eerie race.

"Srexx? You with us, buddy?" Cole asked, breaking the silence after a few moments.

The overhead speakers chirped. "Of course, Cole."

"Access INN's datanet site and download the full broadcast from a news ship in Aurelius. Analyze the living daylights out of it and prepare a report for me once you've done so."

"Yes, Cole," Srexx replied, sounding oddly subdued to Cole's ears, but that was something to investigate later. The overhead speakers chirped again when Srexx 'left' the conversation.

"Garrett, do we need to be in Spark any longer?"

His old friend shook his head. "Not at all, Cole. Any remaining conspirators are of such low level or insignificance that it is unlikely they pose any threat to Spark's overall society. A ship from Beta Magellan can rendezvous with us to take our seventeen prisoners off our hands and deliver them to a prison planet somewhere."

Cole nodded his understanding and slapped the comms control by his right hand, saying, "Cole to Bridge."

The overhead speakers chirped and broadcast, "Bridge, Officer of the Deck."

"Issue immediate recall orders for the battlegroup, and inform Captain Luzader we are departing immediately to investigate an exigent situation. Next, contact Beta Magellan and request two battlegroups meet us in the..." Cole's voice trailed off as he used his implant to access a star chart of the former Commonwealth. "... Diamond system, and tell them to max their hyperdrives. The rendezvous orders are immediate priority. As soon as our battlegroup reports ready, put us on course for Diamond. That's it on my end."

"Very good, sir," the officer of the deck replied. "Consider it done."

Cole nodded, even though the spacer couldn't see him. "Very well. Thank you. Cole out."

The overhead speakers chirped once more, indicating the closed channel.

Leaning back against his seat, Cole couldn't help but concentrate on the cold shiver racing up and down his spine. He could only remember that feeling happening once before, and those events had indelibly etched themselves into his mind. But he supposed one would have that when a joyride in a shuttle leads to one being the sole survivor of a massacred colony.

11

En route to Diamond
Captain's Office, Battle-Carrier *Haven*
12 November 3004

Cole stared at the frozen image hovering above his workstation as he leaned back against his seat. It was a freeze-frame of the full transmission from the INN ship in Aurelius. The sensors on the news ship were barely two grades above the ISA's minimum to be space-worthy, and more than once, Cole had debated the wisdom of releasing the Gyv'Rathi sensor technology to the wild and offering free upgrades to any civilian ship that would make the trip to Gateway or one of Beta Magellan's other holdings. On the one side, the sensors would be a massive improvement for ships… especially their safety.

But two things held him back. First, what other pieces of Gyv'Rathi technology would be necessary for the sensors to work properly? And second, what breakthroughs would the sensors open up once people reverse engineered them?

The last thing Cole wanted was to do something out of a desire for good and have some horrible weapon evolve out of his benevolence. Every time he thought about sharing any Gyv'Rathi tech, the memory of the planet-buster bomb flashed to the forefront of his mind, and a cold shiver ran down his spine. He could only imagine what other tech lurked in the archive.

The hatch irising open was the only warning Cole had before Sasha stormed into his office. Cole turned off the holo-display and gave his first officer his full attention. And she looked like the days had not been kind to her. Dark bags rimmed her eyes, and she was the closest to unkempt Cole had ever seen her.

"Sasha? What's wrong?"

"I can't sleep, Cole. I can't focus on my job. I can't do anything without that news footage flashing through my mind. We need to go to Aurelius. We need to be there... now. Send word to the other battlegroups to meet us there. We can be there in just a couple days if we go to max on the hyperdrive."

The entire time she talked, Sasha paced back and forth like a caged animal, and her hands and fingers flitted about as if no part of her could be still. Cole must not have responded quickly enough to her liking because she stopped pacing and leaned on the edge of his workstation. Her intense stare bored into his soul.

"Please, Cole. I've never asked you for anything. No, wait... I asked you to rescue Talia, which you did, but that's all I've asked you. *Please...* get us to Aurelius as fast as we can; I have to know what's left of my home. Name your price; whatever it is, I'll pay it."

Cole wanted to say 'yes.' The urge to give Sasha whatever she wanted was still strong. If they had still been in an active relationship —personal relationship, that is—he might have said 'yes' without a second thought. But what little sensor data of those unknown ships the news ship included with their broadcast held him back.

"Sasha, please sit. Let's discuss this."

Her desperate, pleading expression shifted to anger in the blink of an eye, and Sasha clenched her fists and slammed them on the workstation. "Dammit, Cole! All you ever do is talk! We need to be in Aurelius *now. I* need to be in Aurelius now. Are you going to take us there or not?"

Cole sighed. "Sasha, you need to take a step back for a second. I never said I wouldn't—"

"Damn you, Cole! Do I have to take command? Is that what it will take? Aurelius needs us, and they need us sooner instead of later!"

Cole held Sasha's gaze and tried to keep his growing concern out of his expression. She wasn't acting like herself. Was this sleep deprivation or something else?

"Srexx," Cole said, "alert Dr. Hrrsh that Sasha will be stopping by for a full medical evaluation, including psych."

The overhead speakers chirped, and Srexx replied, "Yes, Cole. When should Dr. Hrrsh expect her?"

"Within twenty minutes. Thanks, buddy."

The overhead speakers chirped again, and Cole watched Sasha's jaw clench as she curled her hands into fists. "That's not fair, Cole. There's nothing wrong with me."

"Then, Hrrsh's evaluation will prove that."

He watched her stand there, staring at him, and he could see the decision warring within her. She kept teetering back and forth between attacking him. He wasn't telepathic or anything like that; the simple fact was that his time as Jax Theedlow had trained him to be acutely aware of when someone was about to take a swing at him. After all, the spacer haunts that Jax frequented were not usually the kindest places.

When Sasha still warred within herself over the decision several minutes hence, Cole settled the matter. "Go ahead, Sasha. Take a swing. I can see how much you want it, and frankly, you've been rather cool toward me for several weeks now. I don't know where all this is coming from, but if hitting me will help you let it out, go for it. I'll even give you the first one."

Sasha's left fist rose a few millimeters and froze. After a couple more seconds, she growled her anger and frustration before storming out of the office.

"Srexx?"

The overhead speakers chirped, and Srexx said, "Yes, Cole?"

"Monitor Sasha, and if she goes anywhere other than the hospital deck to report to Dr. Hrrsh, notify me at once please."

"Yes, Cole. Is Sasha well? She does not appear to be acting in a manner consistent with what I have come to expect."

He sighed and leaned back against the chair once more. After a couple moments, he shook his head. "I don't know, buddy. I just hope Hrrsh can help her."

LESS THAN AN HOUR LATER, the *other* Thyrray aboard stormed into his office. Cole felt like looking through the hatch to see if Akyra sat at her desk; she didn't seem to be doing a good job of traffic control today.

"Yes, Talia?"

"Why did you order Soosh to report for medical evaluation? Dr. Hrrsh put her on a 72-hour stand-down with partial sedation. Was that your idea?"

Cole pointed to the chairs for visitors and accessed the security feeds for his office. When he found the clip that showed Sasha's visit, he queued it for playback.

"Here," he said, "watch this."

He started the playback, and Talia's ire toward Cole quickly faded. Concern and perhaps sympathy soon dominated her expression. After watching the entire exchange through twice, she collapsed backward against the seat, her demeanor despondent.

"I knew she'd been having a tough time of it since that INN report came in, but I didn't realize it was quite that bad. I've never seen her that close to unhinged, Cole... *never*. Thank you for sending her to Dr. Hrrsh. You may have saved her life."

Cole frowned his lack of understanding and angled his head to one side. "How so?"

"I'd like to think it would never have happened, but if she continued to spiral out, it's not outside the realm of possibility that she might have harmed herself, somehow, or gone rogue. I know people have done worse with less provocation. Ever since we met you, she has always carried a core of guilt that she didn't go back and try to fight the Provisional Parliament in some misguided attempt to save the Commonwealth. We talked about it off and on, and I tried to get her to see it would've been a lost cause. But now this... well, I think the attack on Aurelius tipped the balance."

Cole nodded. "Well, whatever I can do to help, I will. But I won't accelerate our arrival in Aurelius. That would be suicide if that task force is still there. Even with taking three battlegroups, I'm not sure it will be enough."

Now, shock took over Talia's expression. "You're serious? Why do you think that? We've always been the dominant power in this region of space. What makes you think this task force—whoever they are— will be any different?"

Cole accessed his workstation and called up the sensor data from the INN ship and his extrapolations based on that. "Talia, if the sensors on that news ship were even close to accurate, the large ship at the center of that task force is about twenty-five percent larger than *Haven*. Now, Srexx hasn't come back to me yet with his full analysis, but my own surface comparison of the new ship's sensor logs with sensor logs from ships we've captured in battle show an evolutionary similarity in energy weapons... at least to my eyes."

"Evolutionary similarity? I think I know what you mean, but explain please." Talia said.

"Okay. Let's use chemical-based firearms from Old Earth as an example. One of the earliest models was a matchlock, and it may—or may not—have possessed rifling in the barrel. But if you laid one down beside a rifle two—or even three—evolutions newer, you could still see that they were similar devices. Like I said, Srexx hasn't confirmed any of this, but to me, the sensor logs of the unknown ships' energy weapons look like versions of our energy weapons that are several generations more advanced. And if their weapons are more advanced versions of ours, what about their shields? What about their projectile weapons? What about their power generation systems? I am not comfortable going into Aurelius with only three battlegroups, but I don't really have a choice unless I leave the rest of our holdings undefended, except for fixed fortifications like stations and weapons platforms."

"Okay," Talia remarked. "Now, I'm a little worried."

"Welcome to the club," Cole replied. "Want to know more?"

"No… if you don't mind, I think I'm good. I'm sorry I stormed in here like you were to blame for some nefarious scheme… and I'm also sorry Sasha stormed in here acting the way she did. I don't know what has gotten into her."

Cole nodded. "If you don't mind, keep me apprised, please. I can't exactly flip a switch and turn off caring about her."

Talia smiled as she stood and gave an almost-timid nod. "Thank you, Cole. You didn't have to handle her with the kid gloves that you did… not with how she almost attempted mutiny."

"Don't say that, and don't tell anyone what you saw in that clip I showed you. I'm not planning to release it, and if Sasha gets back on an even keel, there's no reason it has to be public knowledge. If it did become public knowledge, I'd probably have to move her out of the fleet. I don't see the people aboard supporting her any longer. And I've already sent a message to Hrrsh that conveyed my concerns without disseminating any specifics."

Talia stepped around Cole's workstation and pulled him into a tight hug. "You're a good man, Cole. Thank you for protecting my sister."

Then, before he could respond, she pivoted and left the office.

Cole remained in his seat as he stared at the closed hatch. Everything he just told Talia was one-hundred-percent true. He didn't want Sasha's conduct to become public knowledge. But that didn't mean he wasn't going to share it with a select group he trusted to keep the matter confidential. And in this case, that 'select group' was a group of one.

He accessed the comms function of his implant and sent a message, then leaned back to wait. No more than ten minutes later, the hatch connecting his office to Akyra's irised open to admit Garrett.

Cole directed Garrett to one of the guest seats and queued up the security footage one more time, saying, "There's something you need to know."

12

Citadel Station
    Beta Magellan
12 November 3004

It was her day off, and Elizabeth spent it wandering the station… as she had spent so many days off since relocating to Beta Magellan. Her sponsor family was great, and if they knew of her background, they didn't show it or treat her any differently than anyone else. Which—frankly—was exactly what she wanted. She didn't *want* her background. What was that saying that was probably older than humans? Something about choosing friends or choosing enemies but not choosing family? Elizabeth wondered how many people who dreamed of having her life would still want it once they knew what it had entailed, and she couldn't comprehend how Cole was as well-adjusted as he was, given everything he survived.

"Hey," a voice drew her out of her thoughts, "you okay?"

Elizabeth turned toward the voice and saw a woman about her age —maybe a few years older—standing a respectful distance away. She wore the uniform of the Haven Protectorate Navy, and faint concern colored her expression.

Elizabeth attempted her best reassuring smile as she said, "Oh, yes, thank you. I was just lost in my thoughts. I'm new here, only relocated to Citadel Station a few weeks ago."

The woman nodded her understanding. "Ah. One of the Kirkland refugees, then?"

Now, it was Elizabeth's turn to nod. "Yes, I was aboard the *Princess Kathryn* and came to Gateway aboard *Haven*."

"You did? What was it like? My friend used to be the weapons officer aboard, and I used to be a junior engineer aboard. I have a bit of crush on that ship; it's so awesome. I know... the other battle-carriers are basically just like it, but *Haven* is special, you know?"

"To be honest, I think I'm still processing everything," Elizabeth replied. "Everything here—from *Haven* to Babylon Station to Citadel Station—is so radically different than anything I'm used to that I think I'm still coming to grips with it."

"Yeah, I get that," the woman responded. Then, her eyes shot wide. "Oh, I am so sorry. Please forgive me. I'm Myrna Mikkel. I work at the shipyard here at Citadel Station."

Elizabeth smiled. "It's nice to meet you. I'm Beth Cavanaugh."

"It's nice to meet you, too. I was on my way to lunch. Would you like to join me?"

"You know... that sounds like an excellent idea," Elizabeth replied. "Thank you for the invitation."

Myrna started walking down the corridor, and Elizabeth fell in beside her. The engineer asked, "So, what do they have you doing here?"

Elizabeth frowned. "Not too much yet, if I'm being honest. I'm still working with my sponsor family, and they told me I wouldn't really progress toward a job until after my orientation."

"Ah. I keep forgetting they do that with refugees now. I came aboard *Haven* in Tristan's Gate... way back in the early, early days. I never went through orientation or anything like that. Beta Magellan wasn't even re-settled yet."

"Oh, wow. So, you're one of the old timers, then?" Elizabeth asked, her expression turning mischievous.

Myrna nudged her with an arm. "Hey, now. I'm not *that* old. I wasn't even out of college yet, but Cole insisted I get my degree. Remote studies was interesting, especially since I was learning *Haven's* systems at the same time I was finishing my degree. And trust me... *Haven's* simplest system makes state-of-the-art for everyone else look like Old Earth marbles or dominoes. There's just no comparing them beyond general function. I mean, life support systems do the same thing, regardless of how they're built... but *Haven's* life support matrix doesn't look anything like 'conventional' life support systems. I'm not sure I could get a job aboard a conventional ship now, regardless of my degree. I'd probably have to start all the way back at a basic Engineering rating and re-learn everything."

Elizabeth smiled to herself as Myrna chattered on, seemingly oblivious to her presence. Myrna asked the occasional question, but overall, she made for pleasant company as they sought lunch.

～

EN ROUTE to Aurelius
Captain's Office, Battle-Carrier *Haven*
20 November 3004

The other two battlegroups arrived in Diamond not too long after *Haven* and her battlegroup did, and Cole was glad they didn't lose too much time waiting on them to arrive. While he didn't share Sasha's sense of almost-frantic urgency on the matter, he wasn't in the mood to sit around twiddling his thumbs, either.

That—or perhaps, *she*—was another reason Cole was glad to be moving toward Aurelius. Matters between him and Sasha had grown even more awkward and strained in the days since her visit to his office. Despite his true thoughts on the matter, Cole was very careful not to frame it as a meltdown or attempted mutiny or insubordination... all of which would have rather unpleasant consequences for Sasha. Social consequences at the very least, if not professional. In looking over their *very* limited interactions over the past eight days, he didn't see how they'd ever get back to where they'd been, and more than once lately, he wondered if maybe the time had come just to call a spade a spade and end it.

But that would leave the matter of her being his first officer. The situation approached dysfunctional at near-lightspeed, and he didn't relish the idea of trying to salvage their professional relationship if the awkwardness that had blossomed between them continued past the termination of their personal relationship. It was a mess, no matter how one sliced it.

The overhead speakers chirped and broadcast Srexx's voice, "Cole? Do you have some time to discuss something?"

"Sure, buddy," Cole replied. "What do you have?"

"Two matters," Srexx answered. "First, I owe you an apology. I have been tracking sensor data since our encounter with the pirates in the Hephaestus system, and I should have notified you at once. However, the data was so unexpected that I have been studying it, and I fear my silence on the matter has led to you being less prepared than you might have been."

Cole leaned back against his seat and considered everything Srexx said. He turned it around in his mind as the silence extended, and after at most ten seconds, he said, "It's about the task force that attacked Aurelius, isn't it?"

"I now evaluate significant odds that it is, yes."

"Well, you know what they say, buddy. Start at the beginning..."

Srexx proceeded to bring Cole up to speed on the Revtamat sensors suddenly delivering data and his study and evaluation of the data, including a plot of the contact's bearing against a star chart of their region of the galaxy ever since the sensors began reporting data. The information that Cole considered to close the case of whether those sensors detected the unknown task force was that the line plotting the bearing to the contact went right through Aurelius at the time the system was attacked.

Cole sat in silence for several moments after Srexx completed the presentation of his first point. He considered everything Srexx had told him and tried to evaluate if his decisions would have been different at all, had Srexx brought this information to his attention sooner. After several minutes, he leaned forward and rested his elbows on his workstation.

"Srexx, buddy, don't worry about not bringing this to me sooner. I can't see how having this information would have changed any of the decisions I made in the intervening weeks, and there was no way for you to know that the sensor data indicated an actual task force in our region of space. All that being said, let's not share this information with Sasha."

"I agree, Cole. I... evaluate that I feel concern for Sasha's well-being. She has not seemed herself since we learned of the attack on Aurelius."

Cole fought the urge to roll his eyes. "Tell me about it. So, that's the first matter. What's the second?"

"I have completed my examination of the INN footage of the attack on Aurelius—and its accompanying sensor data."

It felt like a hollow pit formed in Cole's stomach. Part of him very much did not want to hear this, but he didn't really have much choice if he was going to be the type of person he wanted to be.

"Okay, buddy... lay it on me."

"The sensor systems aboard the news ship were not the best, even when compared to conventional technology, so I am very limited in what I can discern. With that in memory, I evaluate possessing more than sufficient data to state that the task force is an evolution of Gyv'Rathi technology. The ship that most closely matches *Haven* in contours and size does not appear to possess a flight deck or any carrier capability at all, but I share your assessment that the technology displayed bears significant evolutionary similarity to my own. Cole... I am hesitant to predict the outcome of a confrontation between our ships and the task force. I possess insufficient data of any quality to gauge the task force's capability with any accuracy."

Cole sighed. "Yeah... I was expecting that. Are you able to determine if the task force is still in Aurelius?"

"It appears that they have moved on. Calculating the bearing to the sensor contact of the Revtamat sensors yields a line two-point-zero-three-five degrees off our heading to port. Given that we are moving, I cannot determine if the task force is also in transit."

"Right. We'd have to drop out of hyperspace and hold position for a while until you took a new bearing."

"Correct, Cole."

Cole leaned back against his seat again and cracked his knuckles, then rubbed his face with his hands. "We're not doing that. Part of me says we should stop and make damn sure these ships aren't in Aurelius, but people in Aurelius need our relief efforts. Any word on how the rest of the Coalition is responding to the attack?"

"Garrett might be the better to provide this information, but initial reports indicate the vacuum of power at the top of the pyramid has allowed the stress fractures in the overall political entity to surface. There have been upticks in resistance-type activities and communications across most systems of the former Commonwealth and significant increase in their more recent conquests, such as Caernarvon and the former Duchy of Musilar. I do not believe word has reached Kirkland yet, as I have not yet encountered any new information from that region of space."

Cole nodded. "Yeah… Kirkland is a healthy distance from the bulk of the Coalition holdings. I'm not surprised there's no reaction yet. Thanks for all this, buddy. Is there anything else?"

"Not at this time, Cole, and you are welcome."

"All right. Keep me apprised of any new developments, or flag new data for the appropriate person… like Garrett and his people."

"Yes, Cole. Srexx out."

The overhead speakers chirped again, and Cole turned his attention to his workstation. He brought up the comms function and drafted a message to Painter back in Beta Magellan. With the Coalition's apparent flailing in the wake of its leadership's decapitation in Aurelius, there would not be a better time to accelerate their plans to provide financial and material support to the various resistance movements they had established contact with throughout the Coalition.

It was no secret that Beta Magellan was not ready to wage the war of liberation that Cole so strongly wanted, but while Sev and his people worked around the clock to build up the navy and Harlan worked double-time to recruit more marines, there was no reason they couldn't feed the fires of rebellion or revolution as much as they could. After all, any defense assets the resistance movements 'took off the board,' so to speak, were fewer assets Cole and his people would have to capture or destroy when they began liberating systems.

Message complete, Cole sent it and then allowed his mind to drift to the task force and what they represented. For five years, the technology Srexx gifted him in *Haven* and his archives allowed Cole to become the dominant power in the Expansion Zone. But Cole didn't care about power, not in the sense of becoming a galactic overlord. To him, power was much like his vast wealth… a means to an end. What good was all that power and wealth if he didn't use it to help people? To improve people's quality of life?

Sure… to someone on the outside looking in, it probably seemed that Cole was a hypocrite. If he was so interested in improving people's lives, why didn't he release his technology? Except… technology wasn't always the answer. Food. Clothing. Shelter. Safety and Security. Meeting those basic needs did more to lift people up than anything else in existence, and Cole worked to provide a more secure region through the Haven Protectorate.

He chuckled as a memory of an old 2-D movie he watched with his grandfather floated to the surface of his mind. He didn't remember the title… or even much about the movie. Something about world police. He didn't *want* Beta Magellan to be the police of the Expansion Zone. But most systems clawed and scraped for all the resources they could get, and establishing a system defense force—let alone providing freighter escorts or joint security forces—was beyond them.

Despite everything he'd seen during the Jax years—or maybe because of it—Cole had never been one for the 'take care of yourself and devil take the hindmost' mentality. Too many people had helped him—some even without realizing—for him not to help others.

So be it. Cole took a deep breath and slowly exhaled. He didn't relish the thought of facing that task force, but he wasn't about to shrink away from them, either. Too many systems hung in the balance, and his people were the only ones with even a hope of standing up to them.

He pushed himself to stand and left the office. It was time to get to work.

～

THE INCOMING REQUEST for communications became so insistent that it shattered Uxilor's meditative calm. He snarled as he turned his attention to the comms panel near his desk. If this was some other inane matter, he would exterminate whoever disturbed his meditation. He gave explicit orders that he was not to be disturbed.

He slapped the panel with a bit more force than he otherwise might have and growled, "Yes?"

"Sub-Legate, please forgive the interruption, but we just detected a faint hyperdrive signature. It's either right at the edge of our sensor range or the signal is incredibly faint."

A hyperdrive signature? Perhaps, the interruption was warranted after all.

"I forgive you the insubordination. Alter our course to intercept it, but proceed on a cautious approach. After the events of the Aurelius system, I feel the need to be wary for surprises or traps."

"Yes, Sub-Legate."

Uxilor ended the comms call as he felt the ship turn. Good. They already carried out his orders. Finally... they found their quarry at long last. Maybe it wasn't too much to hope that he might return home victorious.

13

Bridge, Battle-Carrier *Haven*
Aurelius System
23 November 3004

Cole watched the system plot populate with data-codes as the sensors teams did their work. Just for laughs, he asked for the archived sensor data to appear beside the current plot, and when that data appeared, he felt a little gut-punched. The current system plot estimated sixty-two percent complete of identifying all contacts in the system, and compared to the plot from their previous visit, Aurelius looked worse than a ghost town.

Several of the ruined hulks of the fleet that 'defended' Aurelius drifted in a loose quasi-orbit around the planet. There was no evidence of the planet's orbital station. None of the asteroid fields bore any data-codes representing active mining operations. System traffic was next to non-existent. At most, a tenth of the planet's human-made satellites remained.

Was this what Sol looked like before humanity transitioned to the stars, minus the ruined hulks of starships? It was a little eerie.

"Helm, plot a least-time course to Aurelius for the battlegroup and upload it to TacNet when ready," Cole said.

Wixil bobbed a nod as she replied, "Yes, Cole!"

Not more than three minutes later, Wixil announced, "Course uploaded."

Less than five minutes after that, Jenkins reported, "All ships signal 'ready,' Cap."

"Go," Cole ordered and successfully fought the urge to add a hand gesture.

On the system plot, he watched the data-codes for the battlegroup start moving deeper into the system. It wasn't long before the sensors teams estimated the system plot was one-hundred-percent up-to-date, and Cole couldn't identify any new information that hadn't been there minutes before. He asked Red to remove the archive plot, as it only served to sadden him at this point.

As the Second Officer, Red should have been in auxiliary control—given that Dr. Hrrsh had extended Sasha's medical stand-down—but for whatever reason, the massive Igthon chose to sit his board at the weapons console. It would be interesting to see what he did if Cole ordered battle-stations.

THE INTERVENING hours that the battlegroup spent going deeper into the system seemed to crawl by for Cole. The current state of the system brought back too many memories. Even though the sensors reported millions of life signs on the planet, Aurelius still felt dead to Cole, and that feeling came perilously close to sending him back to his early teens when he'd looked down upon the smoking remains of his family's colony.

"Orbit achieved, Cole," Wixil announced, drawing Cole out of his thoughts.

"Thank you, Wixil. Haskell, what do you have?"

The senior Sensors spacer remained silent for a few moments before reporting, "Well, Cap... it isn't good. I'm looking at scattered point power sources, couldn't be more than residential generators or batteries. Most of the major urban centers are beyond devastated. There isn't a high-rise over five floors left anywhere on the planet.

And I think I found the main orbital. Sensors report a significant metallic mass at the bottom of this ocean here." The tactical plot shifted to show the ocean in question. "Comparing our scans from the last time we were here to now, I think the tidal waters are still receding in some coastal communities."

Sudden understanding hit Cole, and before he could stop himself, his reaction escaped his lips. "Oh, those bastards... what did they do? Use the station as a kinetic energy weapon?"

"Looks like it, Cap. That station was in one of the planet's LaGrange points. There was no way it would've fallen out of orbit without help."

"Cap," Jenkins said, "we're receiving a general hail. It's using the old colonial era radio frequencies."

"Shit... that might be all they can manage," Cole replied. "Put it on."

The overhead speakers chirped, and static filled the bridge. After a heartbeat or two, the static lessened by about two thirds, and a voice said, "Okay. I think that's got it. Try it now."

Someone cleared his or her throat and said, "Hello. We're sending this broadcast to what we think are a collection of ships just recently arrived in orbit. If you have any medical supplies or foodstuffs to spare, please, help us. Attacks from an unknown force devastated our planet, and we can no longer even provide sufficient food for our surviving population. We..."

The voice faded as the static returned. After a couple seconds, the static ended, and the overhead speakers chirped once more.

"That's all there was, Cap."

"Haskel, can you trace the signal to its source?"

After a couple moments of silence, "Got it, Cap. The broadcast came from what appears to be a ruined military installation. Sensors report several hundred life signs in what's left of the structure but no power signatures to speak of."

Cole sighed. "Jenkins, contact Dr. Hrrsh for a medical crisis response team and Chief Engineer Logan for a team to see about getting a stable power grid up and running. Flight Ops, my compliments to the CAG, if you please; inform her that I will be escorting a medical crisis response team down to the planet and would appreciate a fighter escort. Marine Ops, please pass my compliments to Colonel Devereaux; pass the same message and invite her to send a squad of marines."

The two spacers in the port recess each responded with a crisp, "Aye, sir," making Cole wonder how new they were to his bridge.

Jenkins's response of, "You got it, Cap," was a pleasant counterpoint to the unwanted formality.

Another thought occurred to Cole. "Oh, and Jenkins, fire off a message to Painter back in Beta Magellan, please. Tell her we need to prepare aid convoys for Aurelius."

Minutes became hours, and that passage of time found Cole on the flight deck, watching everything come together for the initial mission to Aurelius. Hrrsh signed off on Sasha accompanying the group, and she had listened to the aborted distress call. At long last, everyone signaled ready to depart, and Cole headed for the shuttle he'd be riding down to the planet. He was no more than halfway to the shuttle when 'Incoming Call - Bridge' appeared in his field of view. He queued his implant to accept the call.

"Cap," Cole heard Red's voice as if the massive Igthon stood in front of him, "we just monitored a hyperdrive footprint at the system periphery. They're here."

Cole nodded, even though Red couldn't see it. Then, said, "Okay. I'll send the shuttles on their way and head back to the bridge. Cole out."

He crossed to the lead shuttle, where Sasha waited. Despite the degradation of their relationship, Sasha could still read him like a billboard. "What's wrong, Cole? What happened?"

"They're back, Sasha. Get these shuttles to planet and do what you can. If we maintain control of the system, relief ships will soon be on the way; I've already sent the message to Painter."

"I should—"

Cole shook his head. "No. Don't think like that. You've been worried about the survivors below ever since we learned of the attack. Go. I'll do what I do, and we'll see about shaking hands on the other side."

Sasha looked like she wanted to say more but settled for a confirmatory nod before she entered the shuttle. Cole stepped back as the ramp rose and locked into position. Moments later, the shuttles and their fighter escorts left the ship, and he headed for the bridge.

"CAPTAIN ON THE BRIDGE!" Red announced as Cole stepped through the inner hatch, and for once, Cole didn't feel like fighting about it.

"Report," he said as he crossed to the command chair and sat.

"We have what appears to be a collection of ships of unknown origin on the system periphery, Cap," Haskel at Sensors said. "Srexx evaluates a ninety-seven-percent probability that these ships are evolutions of the designs present in his schematic archives."

Cole fought the urge to sigh. These ships went through the Coalition fleet that had massed in Aurelius like those Coalition ships weren't even there. While he didn't think his ships would be quite so easy to defeat, he would've been lying if he said he wasn't concerned at all.

"Helm, plot an intercept course for the unknown ships. If they force an engagement, I want the fight to happen well away from Aurelius."

"Yes, Cole," Wixil replied. No more than five minutes later, "Course plotted and uploaded to TacNet."

"Thank you, Wixil," Cole said. "Form up the battlegroup, and let's head out."

A LITTLE OVER fifteen hours later, the battlegroup met the unknown ships. Cole attempted to hail them at various points during the journey to meet them across every possible frequency and medium... all with no response.

The overhead speakers chirped and broadcast Srexx's voice, "Cole?"

"Yeah, buddy?"

"I have concluded my analysis. These ships are evolutionarily derivative of the designs and technology we possess through my archives. It would appear that they are Gyv'Rathi in origin, but I am concerned at their lack of response. I have attempted to communicate with them using various methods that would not translate well to you, but like your attempts, I have not received a response. Based on their observed conduct in this system, I was hoping they were *not* my creators. I do not... like... that they have fallen so far that they do as they have done."

Cole frowned as he considered Srexx's information. "What if they're not Gyv'Rathi?"

"I do not understand, Cole."

"If they're not behaving as you would expect for Gyv'Rathi, that—to me—leads to the possible conclusion that they're *not* Gyv'Rathi. Now, granted, thirty-five thousand years is a long time for societal shifts and moral re-evaluations, but is it possible whoever's flying those ships are not the Gyv'Rathi?"

"That presents an interesting conundrum, Cole. I had not considered that. I shall re-double my efforts to obtain access to their systems. They have proven frustratingly secure thus far."

"Energy surge! I think they're charging weapons, Cap!" Haskell at Sensors announced.

"Sound battle stations," Cole replied. "Bring up the tactical plot."

Moments later, Cole thought he felt something through the soles of his feet.

"Outer shield layer down five percent," Red reported. "It appeared to be a single energy weapon discharge from the ship roughly matching our dimensions, Cap."

Cole leaned back against his seat and put effort into maintaining his non-expression. But he was just a bit unsettled. Five percent? Off of one weapon? This was going to be interesting.

"Alert Engineering to bring the generator up to one-hundred-five percent and divert the additional power to shields," Cole replied.

Jenkins announced, "Message coming in!"

Cole nodded. "Play it."

The main viewer at the front of the bridge activated, as the overhead speakers chirped, and Cole blinked at the sight. The 'people' in view looked roughly humanoid, except they bore what appeared to be a kind of chitinous exoskeleton. Two arms left upper shoulders and ended in hands with three thick digits and an equally thick opposable thumb, while two more sets of limbs that looked more like spider legs attached to their torsos below their arms.

"I am Sub-Legate Uxilor," the person in the center of the view said. "If you surrender the Gyv'Rathi battleship and all ships you have constructed using its technology, we may permit your pathetic existence to continue."

"Cole," Srexx said, "you were correct. These are *not* Gyv'Rathi. They are a quasi-insectoid race that call themselves the Tovasq, and my creators confronted them at multiple points throughout the historical records I have."

Cole nodded. "So, they're not Gyv'Rathi. That actually makes me feel better about all this. Jenkins, record for transmission please."

"You're on, Cap."

"Hello, Uxilor. I'm Cole, and I have to say that I dispute your evaluation that our existence is pathetic. Furthermore, you present no evidence or anything really that you have any authority to order us to surrender these ships. And so... to paraphrase someone from my people's ancient past, come and take them."

Moments later, Jenkins reported, "Ready to transmit, Cap."

"Send it," Cole replied.

The Tovasq replied with general weapons fire from every ship along their 'line.'

"Shield damage across the targeted ships," Red reported. "No damage beyond that."

"All ships, weapons free for your size class and below; leave the battleship for *Haven* and her sister ships. Flight Ops, signal 'Red Deck' to the CAG, if you please; I want to know that the fighters won't be fodder for their point defense before we launch."

As the formations closed the range between them, ships on both sides began flashing yellow as they exchanged weapons fire. Cole actually chose to activate the force-field restraints for the command chair as the deck beneath him began heaving to such a degree that remaining seated became a challenge. As the minutes passed, more and more of Cole's smaller ships—the frigates and destroyers—shifted from green to yellow to red to the occasional gray, but they gave as good as they got. The smaller ships of the task force shifted from yellow to red to gray as well.

It became a battle of attrition, and while Cole's ships outnumbered the Tovasq by almost a factor of three, the Tovasq ships represented the culmination of thirty-five-thousand years of further refinement and technological development.

Haven was into her third shield layer when Cole saw an opening appear in the coverage between his fleet and the Tovasq battleship. Every instinct shouted at him that he needed to capitalize, and he called out, "Wixil, spearhead! Jenkins, have the other battle-carriers fall in behind us. I want that big bastard out of the fight. Red, light off the broadsides along the way."

Cole watched the shields drop by fives and tens as *Haven* led the way into the enemy formation as he had done so many times before, and as the deck beneath him bucked like a dinghy in a hurricane, he consider that *perhaps* spearhead may not have been the truly wisest choice. But the decision was made, and the only way out was through.

Faced with the battleship-grade broadsides—even as comparatively ancient as they were—the smaller ships could not hold out, especially while fending off the combined attacks of their counterparts as well. Cole watched the field of gray on the tactical plot expand as *Haven* forced her way deeper into the enemy formation.

The Tovasq battleship concentrated its fire on *Haven*, seemingly aware that she was the primary threat, and *Haven*'s shields evaporated under its full assault. The crew around Cole announced damage reports, but he tuned them out. His sole focus was maintaining the pressure on the battleship until *Haven*'s sisters could lend their weight to the fight.

The lights flickered. Panels exploded, showering nearby spacers with sparks. Cole ordered maneuvers to keep *Haven* in the fight, watching as she battered her opponent just as her opponent battered her. The other two battle-carriers slid into position around the battleship, adding their fire to both the battleship and the surrounding small ships.

But the battleship fought on, focusing all its fire on *Haven*.

A massive explosion rocked the bridge, throwing Cole hard to his right. Lights all over the bridge erupted in sparks and went dark. Another explosion. One of the decking panels by the command chair heaved upward and failed under extreme stress, slapping the command chair—and Cole—aside like a toddler having a tantrum.

14

Cole opened his eyes and winced at the bright light around him. He blinked, and his surroundings came into focus. He was in a hospital room. There were no specific markings to tell him *which* hospital, though. Was he still aboard *Haven*?

The hatch in the far corner irised open to admit a woman wearing a shipsuit with the ages-old symbol of human medicine on the left shoulder. Cole didn't recognize her, or at least, he didn't *think* he recognized her.

"Good morning, Mister Coleson," she said as she stopped at the foot of his bed. "I'm Doctor Hansen, and we are very glad that you decided to return to us."

"Where am I?" Cole asked, his voice raspy from dehydration and lack of use.

The woman maintained a pleasant smile as she answered, "Citadel Station. You've been here for a little over a week now, and you have a few people waiting to see you if you feel up to it."

Cole frowned as he took stock of himself. He didn't feel bad, per se, but he was lying on a bed. He shrugged and felt no ill effects. Then, lifted his arms and wiggled his toes. Everything seemed to work as it should. He sat up in bed and felt no headache, nor did the room spin.

"Okay. Sure. I guess I feel fine enough."

Doctor Hansen smiled. "Excellent. Give me just a moment."

She stepped outside, and not even moments later, Wixil, Yeleth, Mazzi, and Garrett entered the room… with Doctor Hansen close behind them. Wixil surged up onto the bed and snuggled close to Cole, and he fought the urge to grin at the sound and feel of her deep purr as she enfolded him in a tight hug.

"Since I'm alive and back in Beta Magellan, I'm guessing we won?" Cole asked.

"We defeated the task force," Mazzi replied. "I'm still not sure we won. Over half of our ships didn't come home under their own power, including *Haven*. I'm afraid she's beat to scrap, Cole."

Cole's eyes shot wide. "Srexx? Is he—"

Speakers in the room chirped and broadcast a very welcome voice, "I am here, Cole. When we have some time, I should probably make a few confessions to you that I had neglected to mention previously. Suffice to say, however, the destruction of *Haven* did not threaten my existence. I am also rather pleased with the data we recovered from the remains of the task force. Knowing that the crew of the ships were Tovasq has assisted in my efforts to decrypt and translate the data. I have only spent a little over one week on the process, though, and I evaluate it will be some time yet before I have any meaningful information for you."

"That's fine, buddy," Cole replied, relaxing to an easy smile. "I'm just glad you're still with us. What of Aurelius and Sasha?"

Mazzi did a good job of mostly hiding her wince. "Sasha elected to remain on Aurelius, Cole. She's leading the recovery efforts there. So, it seems like the Tovasq crushed the bulk of the upper echelons of the Coalition command structure during their first trip through Aurelius, and these last couple weeks, systems all across Coalition space are rising up in rebellion. I'd say by this time next year, the Coalition will be little more than a bad memory."

"Good," Cole remarked. "Let's do what we can to help that along. How's Painter doing on the relief convoys to Aurelius?"

"The first one should have arrived yesterday," Garrett answered, "and the equivalent of a system picket accompanied it to maintain system security while we help them rebuild. We have also recovered as much of the Tovasq task force as we can, so between our research departments and Srexx's efforts, it'll be interesting to see what we can piece together in terms of technology upgrades."

Cole nodded. "Send word to Sev. I don't want him starting on a new *Haven* until we have a chance to see what—if any—improvements the Tovasq ships reveal. I think, for now, I'll concentrate on shoring up things here in Beta Magellan. Doctor, when can I leave?"

Doctor Hansen stepped around the group as she said, "Your scans all appear good. Let's try standing and walking a short distance, and if you don't exhibit any concerns, I see no reason you can't leave right now."

As MONTHS PASSED, the collapse of the Coalition accelerated as word spread far and wide that its leaders were no more. The Haven Protectorate didn't expand—as such—but more than a few systems received a system picket or home fleet from Beta Magellan when they asked for one.

A few years later, Cole shocked the 'upper crust' of galactic society when he married some no-name refugee—some woman named Elizabeth Cavanaugh—and for some reason, anyone from Beta Magellan always seemed amused by that reaction. Little more than a year after the happy couple announced their marriage, they announced the arrival of a daughter, and many people breathed a sigh of relief that Cole finally had an heir... well... heiress.

The turmoil of the recent past faded as more and more societies of the former Coalition emerged from their dark night and resumed trade and contact with the Expansion Zone at large. Despite the occasional disagreement, though, relative peace reigned. It seemed no one felt it wise to risk drawing the attention of Beta Magellan... or its new flagship, the dreadnought *Haven II*.

WHAT'S NEXT?

Have you read "Ships in the Night," the story of Cole's first adventure as Jax Theedlow?

If not, sign up for my newsletter to get it.
https://click.knightsfallpress.com/cole-srexx

~

This concludes the Cole & Srexx series.

Thank you for following Cole and his friends throughout their adventures.

ACKNOWLEDGMENTS

There's an old saying: it takes a village to raise a child. I don't know if that's true or not, but it certainly seems true where publishing a story is concerned. You would not be reading this were it not for contributions from several people.

The editor of this work, T. F. Poist, deserves far more than a simple 'thank you' for her efforts with this work. Her time, knowledge, and expertise improved this work beyond measure.

Did you like the cover? The background image was created by Jakub Skop (https://www.behance.net/JakubSkop).

I'm sure there are many who will see this next paragraph and think, "Goodness, he's acknowledging his parents and grandparents *again?*" My greatest regret is that I cannot hand my grandfather, Bob Miller, a paperback copy of my novels. So, yes...the Acknowledgements page of *every* story I publish will have the paragraph that follows. Consider yourselves forewarned.

Without my grandparents, Bob & Janice Miller, I honestly don't know where I'd be today; my grandfather taught me to read and love reading, and my grandmother taught me to develop and exercise my imagination. This story (not to mention my life in general) certainly would not have happened without my parents, Vernon & Judy Kerns.

THE WORLDS OF ROBERT M. KERNS

For a complete and accurate listing of all publications, both currently available and forthcoming, please visit Knightsfall Press.

Knightsfall Press - Books

https://knightsfall.press/books

SO... WHO'S THE AUTHOR?

Robert M. Kerns (or Rob if you ever meet him in person) is a geek, and he claims that label proudly. Most of his geekiness revolves around Information Technology (IT), having over fifteen years in the industry; within IT, he especially prefers Servers and Networks, and he often makes the claim that his residence has a better data infrastructure than some businesses.

Beyond IT, Rob enjoys Science Fiction and Fantasy of (almost) all stripes. He is a voracious reader, with his favorite books too numerous to list.

Rob has been writing for over 20 years, published his first novel in 2018, and has no plans to stop any time soon.

Connect with Rob at robertmkerns.com.

facebook.com/RobertMKerns

amazon.com/author/robertmkerns

bookbub.com/authors/robert-m-kerns